D1373238

Mango Blues

A Mango Bob and Walker Adventure

by

Bill Myers

www.mangobob.com

This book is a work of fiction. Names, characters, places and incidents are either the product of the author's imagination or are used fictionally. Any resemblance to actual persons, living or dead, or to actual events or locales is entirely coincidental.

This book is licensed for your personal enjoyment only. This book may not be re-sold or given away to other people. If you would like to share this book with another person, please purchase an additional copy for each person you share it with.

Copyright © 2017 Bill Myers. All rights reserved including the right to reproduce this book or portions thereof, in any form. No part of this text may be reproduced in any form without the express written permission of the author.

Version 2017.01.15

Chapter One

I knew there would be trouble when I saw her step out of the car. She looked to be about sixteen and maybe six months pregnant. A lit cigarette in one hand, an open beer in the other.

I didn't know who she was and shouldn't have cared.

But I did.

I watched another girl climb out after her. This one a bit older. Dirty blonde hair cut short. A skirt showing too much leg, a skull tattoo on her shoulder. Laughing and drinking and pointing at the pregnant girl's belly.

They were in an old Chevy Suburban. Dusty brown, sagging springs, out of state plates. Two aluminum ladders strapped to the roof rack.

An older woman, maybe the girl's mother, got out on the driver's side. Beer in hand, wearing a bikini top and hot pink stretch pants.

She looked over at us in the motorhome, nodded slightly, then turned her attention back to the two girls. She said something that made them look in our direction and laugh. Then the three of them turned and headed across the parking lot toward the dollar store.

When they reached the front door, the pregnant girl put her beer on top of the trash can by the door, stubbed her cigarette out on the sidewalk and went inside.

The two other women stayed outside finishing off their

beers.

I turned to Kat. "You see that?"

She nodded but didn't say anything.

"That girl shouldn't be smoking. She's pregnant."

Kat nodded again but said nothing.

"Someone should talk to her. It won't be good for the baby."

Kat smiled.

We were traveling across Florida in my motorhome. Kat, me, and Mango Bob, my bobtailed cat. We were staying on the back roads because Kat wanted to avoid the interstates. "Too many cars," she'd said. "Too many people knowing our business."

I wasn't sure why she was worried about people 'knowing our business'. We weren't up to anything illegal, just heading for a campground somewhere north of Cedar Key.

It was Kat's idea. She'd reminded me that I'd been promising to teach her to drive the motorhome and today was the day. She planned out the route we were to follow and told me when we needed to leave.

Normally, I would have asked questions. But being single, unemployed and having plenty of free time on my hands, I wasn't going to miss out on the opportunity to spend a few days with the lovely Kat in my motorhome.

So far, we were just friends. Not sleeping together or anything. But there was always hope. So when she asked me to take her camping for a few days, I jumped at the chance.

Looking back, I should have known something was up.

Chapter Two

I'd only known her for about a month. We'd met while I was in Key West; I'd gone there to help out a friend who was having a problem. I'm doing that a lot of lately. Helping friends who've run into problems. Usually the kind of problems where you don't want to get the cops involved.

My name's Walker and, until I was fired, I was happily living the corporate life working computer security for a Fortune 100 company. I'd moved up the ladder into a management position. It came with all the perks. A company car, big salary and a nice pension plan.

But all that went away when I was fired. I'd been running some reports on the company's mainframe and had found some major discrepancies in the corporate financials. When I presented my findings to the board, they blamed me for the problem and fired me.

That left me with no income, no job prospects and not enough cash to make house payments or pay rent. Looking for a quick solution, I sold everything I had, bought a ten-year-old motorhome and hit the road.

Two months later, the company offered me a fairly large monetary settlement. All I had to do was forget about the discrepancies I'd found. For me, it was a no brainer. I took their money and never looked back.

With plenty of cash in the bank, I drove the motorhome to Florida and found a nice place just south of Sarasota to park it near the beach. In the year since, I've made some good friends, met a few women and stayed semi busy doing freelance computer work.

I could probably find a full-time job if I looked for one, but since I don't need the money and like the freedom of living and traveling in my motorhome, I'm not looking for work. But sometimes work finds me. That's why I was in Key West. And that's where I met Kat.

She was a friend of a friend. Her full name is Katrina. I learned early on never to call her that. It's Kat or get punched. She's three or four years younger than me, which puts her in her late twenties. Medium height, maybe five foot seven, a little on the skinny side.

Auburn hair, cut short. Always dresses Key West casual— baggy shorts and a T-shirt. The day I met her, she was wearing a tight fitting white one with a Smith & Wesson logo on it. I liked what I saw.

They tell me she's a Russian princess. Don't know if she is or not, but she's definitely got the looks. She doesn't handle herself like royalty though. More like a hit man for the mob. In fact, some people think she is, especially those who know her father. It was at his request that Kat left Key West with me. He said it was a good time for her to lay low until things cooled off in the Keys. He wasn't talking about the weather.

The plan was she'd come back to my home base in Englewood and I'd teach her how to drive a motorhome. Then I'd help her find one to buy. Her daddy would be putting up the money. After she got a motorhome, she'd travel around in it a bit until it was safe to return to Key West.

It wasn't my plan, it was her father's. But since it wasn't going to cost me any money and I'd get to spend time with

Kat, it sounded good to me.

The living arrangements were worked out before we left —she wouldn't be staying with me in my motorhome. Not that I wouldn't enjoy it, but her father wasn't keen on the idea. He'd made a call and was able to rent a trailer in the same RV park I called home. A place just two doors down from me. Close enough that I could keep an eye on her, but far enough away that we wouldn't be tempted to get too cozy after dark.

When it came to the 'getting cozy' part of the plan, Kat had a different idea.

Chapter Three

We left around ten in the morning. Because we had to go through the congested construction zones around the new mall they were building in Sarasota and then into Tampa's heavy traffic, Kat wanted me to drive the first leg.

I didn't mind. In fact, I would have suggested it if she hadn't. The construction zone on I-75 had concrete barriers on the left and right shoulders, narrowing the lanes and requiring a steady hand on the wheel. Misjudge the width by a few inches and the side of the motorhome would be scraping concrete. It would be an expensive repair.

Kat was fine with me driving. She was happy to sit back and watch me steer the big motorhome through heavy traffic, trying to keep it between the concrete barriers. She said she'd take the wheel when we got to the Sun Coast Parkway on the other side of Tampa. There'd be a lot less traffic and easier driving there.

She'd driven my motorhome once before, back when we were in Key West. But not with my permission. I'd stepped out and left the keys in the ignition. She decided that would be a good time to take it out for a test drive.

It was pouring rain and the slick and narrow roads outside of Key West almost got the better of her. After a few close calls, she came to her senses, parked the motorhome and waited for me to come get her.

Today would be different. She'd be driving with my

blessing. The road she'd be on, the Sun Coast Parkway, was a well maintained divided highway with almost no traffic. The weather was perfect, blue skies and no wind. All we needed to do was get through the craziness of Tampa traffic.

While I was trying to do that, she fiddled with the GPS and occasionally responded to text messages on her phone. After one of these messages, she pointed to the GPS and asked, "It says we'll get there around one. You think that's right?"

I didn't know what she'd entered as our destination, so wasn't sure where we'd be going. But I knew from previous trips that the arrival time shown on the GPS was pretty accurate—usually within a few minutes, assuming no major problems on the road.

"Yeah, it's probably close. What'd you put in as our destination?"

"Crystal River. I figured we could stop there and eat lunch."

Sounded good to me. Crystal River was about half way to Manatee Springs State Park. That's where Kat said we'd be camping for the night.

Leaving Tampa traffic behind, I took the Water Avenue exit and pulled into the Wawa parking lot. Normally, I'd want to stop and get one of Wawa's fresh sandwiches or maybe a burrito. But not today. It was too early for lunch and we were on a mission.

I pulled through the lot and found a safe place to park near the back exit. I left plenty of space in front of the motorhome, trying to make it easy for Kat to get us back out on the road. I put the motorhome in park and looked over at her. "You ready?"

She nodded. "As ready as I'll ever be."

I moved to the passenger seat and Kat took her place behind the wheel. She fiddled with the mirrors and the seat until she got them the way she wanted then she looked at me and nodded. She was ready.

I buckled my seat belt and hoped for the best.

She revved the engine, shifted into drive and pulled out into traffic. She caught the first red light and rolled to a stop. When the light changed to green, she moved over into the right lane. A car behind us honked, probably mad that she'd cut him off. She ignored the honker and made her way to the on ramp taking us back on the highway.

The motorhome was slow getting up to speed, giving the car behind us, the one that had honked, a chance to pass. It was a late model Mustang, white with dark tinted windows and growling exhaust. When it went by, the driver stuck his hand out the window and gave Kat a one finger salute. She smiled and asked, "A friend of yours?"

I ignored her. I didn't want to distract her while she was driving the motorhome. Nothing to gain and too much to lose.

She stayed in the far right lane and slowly brought the motorhome up to cruising speed. For the first few minutes she kept a death grip on the wheel, holding on tight in case something went wrong.

Nothing did. The motorhome was large, slow to get up speed and took more room to stop than a car. But it was fairly easy to drive, especially when the roads were good and there was little traffic.

Kat quickly got the hang of it and it wasn't long before she had a smile on her face and the look of someone who was clearly enjoying the drive. That lasted for about two hours, just enough time for us to reach the end of the Sun Coast

Parkway and enter the stop and go traffic of Crystal River.

When Kat saw that the parking lot at the dollar store was almost empty and big enough for the motorhome, she pulled in. She found an open space at the edge of the lot and parked. She turned off the motor and turned to me. "How'd I do?"

It was easy for me to answer. She'd gotten us to Crystal River safe and sound. No close calls, no panic stops, no dents or scratches. I couldn't ask for much more.

"You did good. You got us here safe and sound. The only thing you need to work on is your stops. It takes longer to stop the motorhome than a car, so you have to get on your brakes a little earlier."

She smiled. "Yeah, I noticed that. I'll keep that in mind next time I drive."

She nodded toward the dollar store. "Anything you need in there?"

"No. How about you?"

"I think I'm set. You ready for lunch?"

I was. We'd stocked the fridge with sandwich fixings and cold drinks before we'd left. Our plan was to eat in the motorhome no matter where we were. It was Kat's idea. She said she didn't want to risk getting food poisoning eating out. I couldn't blame her. I'd had food poisoning before and it wasn't fun.

Keeping with Kat's plan, we made turkey sandwiches and opened a tube of chips. She was drinking iced tea out of a bottle and I had a Mountain Dew. We were sitting at the motorhome's dinette table, Kat on one side, me on the other. Between us, at the end of the table, a large window gave us a long view of the dollar store parking lot.

That's when we first noticed them. They pulled up and parked between us and the store. No other cars around. Just them. From our vantage point, we watched the pregnant girl climb out of the SUV with cigarette in hand. We saw her mother hand her a beer. And then we watched as they made their way to the front of the store.

I nodded in the girl's direction. "Someone needs to talk to her. Tell her she doesn't need to be smoking or drinking when she's pregnant."

Kat nodded. "You're right. When she comes back out of the store, I'll do it."

Chapter Four

After the pregnant girl had gone into the store, the two women who were with her went back to the Suburban. Instead of getting in, they walked around to the back of the big SUV, opened the lift gate and cleared out room to sit.

With the lift open, we could see what they had inside—several cardboard boxes, a couple of beat up suitcases and a large, white ice chest. The older woman, the one who had been driving, opened the ice chest. She pulled out a beer and popped the top. She took a drink, looked in our direction and smiled.

It was the second time she'd looked our way and smiled. Almost like she knew who we were. But there was no way she could see us, the side windows in the motorhome were heavily tinted, including the one nearest us. They were designed so that we could see out but no one could see in. Maybe the woman knew someone who had a motorhome that looked like mine, and maybe she thought that was who we were. But we weren't. I didn't know her and I doubted Kat did.

A few minutes later, the pregnant girl came out of the dollar store carrying a small shopping bag. She walked to the Suburban and said something to the older woman. Whatever she'd said seemed to make her happy. She opened the ice chest and handed the pregnant girl a beer.

Kat saw the beer and said, "That's enough of that. I'm going to go talk to her. You stay here."

She stood and headed for the door but I stopped her. Someone did need to talk to the girl, tell her that smoking and drinking while she was pregnant wasn't a good idea, but I wasn't sure it should be Kat who did the talking. The trio at the back of the SUV might take offense at a stranger lecturing them on their lifestyle choices. I know I would.

"Kat, maybe we just leave it alone. Let someone else do it."

She shook her head. "No. I'm not going to wait for someone else to do it. Today it's going to be me."

I knew better than to argue with her, so I said, "If you're going over there, I'm going with you."

Again, she shook her head. "No. You stay here. It'll be easier for me to talk to them woman to woman. If I drag a man over there, they'll go on the offensive. So you just stay here and watch. If things get out of hand, you can come rescue me."

That made me laugh. Kat wasn't the type of person who ever needed rescuing. She had proven she could take care of herself. Armed or unarmed, she could handle the situation. If things got out of hand, it would be the three women who needed rescuing.

Still, I didn't like staying behind. But what Kat said made sense. It might be easier for a woman to talk to another woman about pregnancy without a man around.

She reached for the door and said, "Wish me luck."

Chapter Five

The three women saw Kat coming across the parking lot. The older one, the one I figured was the mom, set her beer on the ice chest, stood up and took the stance of a fighter. Head tilted down, eyes looking forward, clinched fists held in front of her face. The two girls with her moved back a few steps, giving their mom plenty of room to rumble.

If it was a rumble she wanted, Kat was going to give it to her. She lowered her head, focused her eyes on the woman's face and walked straight at her. It looked like a fight was inevitable. But I couldn't figure out why.

Kat hadn't said a word to any of the women. She'd simply gotten out of the motorhome and headed in their general direction. For all they knew, she was taking a short cut across the parking lot to get to the dollar store.

But somehow Kat had triggered a fight response in the older woman. She clearly saw Kat as a threat, someone who might harm her daughters. Like a mama bear protecting her cubs, she was ready for battle.

The whole thing seemed crazy to me. Kat didn't know this woman and the woman didn't know her. If the woman *had* known Kat, she'd know better than to pick a fight with her.

It happened quickly. Kat was four steps away when the older woman dropped her fists and turned to the Suburban. She opened the ice chest and pulled out a cold beer. She turned back around and offered it to Kat.

Kat refused the beer and instead grabbed the woman in a bear hug. With her arms tightly wrapped around the woman, Kat leaned in and whispered something. Then she released her hold and took a step back. I expected the older woman would take a swing at Kat, but she didn't. Instead, she pointed at the motorhome and laughed.

The two younger girls came up behind Kat and hugged her one at a time. They were smiling and laughing and it looked like a family reunion. Kat patted the pregnant girl's belly and wagged her finger at the beer can she was holding, apparently telling her it wasn't a good idea to drink when pregnant.

Kat had a short conversation with the mom. I couldn't hear what they were saying, but after it was over they were both still smiling and no punches had been thrown. The mom walked over to the passenger side of the Suburban, opened the door and pulled out a dark green duffel bag, the kind that returning soldiers bring back with them from the battlefield.

She carried the duffel to the back of the Suburban and put it on the ground in front of the pregnant girl. She said a few words to her and they hugged. Then the older girl came over and hugged the pregnant girl. When all the hugging was done, Kat picked up the duffel and she and the pregnant girl walked away from the Suburban. They headed toward the motorhome.

Behind them, the mom and the other girl got in their Suburban and drove off. I wasn't sure what was going on, but with Kat and the pregnant girl getting closer to the motorhome I was about to find out.

I met them at the door.

Kat spoke first. "Walker, this is Ricki. She's going to be riding with us for a while."

Ricki smiled, held out her hand, and in the singsong voice of a young girl said, "Glad to meet you, Mr. Walker. Mind if I come in?"

I did mind, but there was no way I could refuse her. A young pregnant girl standing out in the hot Florida sun wasn't someone you turn away. It was cool in the motorhome and I invited her in. I only hoped her stay would be short.

She climbed in and Kat followed. The girl looked around and said, "This is nice. Is this yours?"

I nodded. "Yeah, it's mine. I live in it full time."

"Really? I'd love to do that. Live in a motorhome, go anywhere I wanted. Not have to worry about anyone else. Just me."

I looked at her pregnant belly and thought, *'no, it wouldn't be fun to be pregnant and traveling alone in a motorhome. And it wouldn't be just you. Soon you'd have a baby to take care of'.* And Anyway, she looked too young to have a driver's license. I was tempted to bring this up, but before I could, she saw Bob coming up from the back.

"You have a cat?"

I decided to play nice.

"Yeah, I do. I guess he heard your voice and decided to come check you out."

His stump of a tail twitched back and forth as he sniffed Ricki's shoe. He was trying to decide whether she was good or evil. Bob had known a lot of people. Most had been good, but not all. The ones that had treated him badly when he was young had made him cautious. As a first line of defense, he sniffed the shoes of newcomers to judge them. If he smelled evil, his ears would fold back, he'd hiss and go hide.

With Ricki, he did neither. She'd passed his test. He rubbed up against her ankle and let out a soft "Meow." His way of saying, "Give me some loving."

"He's sweet," she said. "What's his name?"

"Bob, short for Mango Bob."

"Mango Bob? I like it. It suits him. How long have you had him?"

I didn't mind talking about Bob and I'm sure he liked the attention, but what I really wanted to know was why a young pregnant girl had joined us in the motorhome. I didn't want to upset her, so I answered her question.

"Bob's been with me about a year."

She rubbed his stump of a tail. "What happened here?"

"He's an American bobtail. They're born with little, stubby tails like that."

She nodded. "Kind of makes him look like a bobcat. Does he bite?"

I smiled. "He bites his food. But I've never seen him bite a person."

She bent down to rub his back. Her pregnant belly pushed up against him as she got close. For some reason, this spooked Bob. He stood, shook off invisible demons and ran to the back.

We stood in silence, watching as he sped away. He disappeared into the back bedroom, one of his favorite hiding places. His other favorite place was the bathroom. That's where I kept his food, water and litter box.

Ricki broke the silence with a question. "Mind if I use your bathroom?"

I hadn't had much experience around pregnant women, in fact, none at all. But I'd heard they needed frequent bathroom breaks. The bathroom in the motorhome was in the back, across from the bedroom. It had everything a regular bathroom had, but on a smaller scale. I'd cleaned it for the trip, so it had that going for it.

"Feel free to use it, it's in the back."

She grabbed her duffel bag and dragged it back to the bathroom with her. After she'd closed the door, I turned to Kat. "Care to explain what's going on?"

She smiled. "She needed a ride. I offered her one."

"I get that. But she's pregnant. She looks pretty far along. You think it's safe for her to be traveling with us? What if the baby comes?"

Kat smiled and put her hand on my shoulder. "Walker, don't worry about the baby. It won't be a problem."

I wasn't so sure. Traveling with a stranger, a pregnant one at that, sure didn't seem like a good idea to me.

Kat and I were still standing near the front of the motorhome quietly talking about having a pregnant girl traveling with us. I was facing away from the back when I heard the toilet flush and the bathroom door open.

Not wanting to be rude, I didn't turn to look. But I should have. The pregnancy was no longer an issue.

Chapter Six

"Did you tell him yet?"

The voice asking the question wasn't the same singsong voice of the young girl who'd gone into the bathroom. It was different. Stronger, deeper, more confident.

I turned and, instead of seeing the pregnant teenaged girl, I saw an attractive woman. Maybe in her late twenties, early thirties. Short, spiky hair; slim, athletic build. Five foot tall and definitely not pregnant.

She didn't look much like the girl who had gone into the bathroom, but it had to be her. Somehow she'd changed into an adult in the few minutes she'd been in there. I had a lot of questions starting with, "Where's the baby?"

Instead of answering, the Joan Jett lookalike pointed at Kat. "Ask her."

I wasn't sure why she wanted me to ask Kat to answer the question, but if that's what it took, that's what I was going to do.

I turned to Kat. "Tell me what's going on."

She smiled. "Walker, this is my friend Devin. As you can probably tell, she's not a teenager and she's not pregnant. And no, she didn't have the baby in your bathroom.

"She called me this morning and said she had a package for my father. The kind of package you can't send through the mail. She said I needed to come up here and pick it up in person. I didn't want to do it alone, so I asked you."

This was typical Kat. She hadn't answered the question I'd asked. Instead, she'd given me an answer to a question I should have asked hours earlier, like why she was in such a hurry to get on the road that morning. It wasn't that she wanted to spend a few days camping with me in the motorhome. It had to do with a package she was supposed to pick up and deliver to her father.

This wasn't the first time I'd been fooled by a woman. Probably wouldn't be the last. But with Kat, I expected better. There was no reason not to tell me the truth about the trip. If she'd told me we needed to drive to Crystal River to pick up a package, it wouldn't have been a big deal. I would have been happy to do it. But she hadn't told me about the package, and that usually meant there were other secrets yet to be told. Like, "What's the deal with the pregnant girl who is no longer pregnant?"

I asked once and didn't get an answer. I asked again. "So there's a package we're supposed to pick up for your dad. I don't have a problem with that. But how does your friend here pretending to be a pregnant teen fit in with that?"

This time it was Kat who pointed. She aimed her finger at Devin, her no longer pregnant, no longer teenager friend. "You tell him."

I'd seen this before. Two women tag teaming me. First one side of the story then the other. Telling me only what they wanted me to hear with a lot of important details left out—like why I was sitting in a dollar store parking lot a long way from home with a stranger about to tell me stories.

I wanted to hear what she had to say. I didn't expect it to be the truth, but it had the potential of being entertaining—what with the fake pregnancy and the teen disguise.

Since I figured it might take a while to hear it out, I

pointed at the couch. No need for us to stand through the whole thing. Might as well get comfortable.

Devin took a seat and Kat sat down beside her. I moved to the lounge chair across from them and waited for the storytelling to begin. Devin started with a question. "Do you have something I can drink?"

I nodded. "Yeah, we have water. Will that do?"

Water wasn't the only thing we had. But it was the only thing I wanted to offer her until I heard her story.

"Water will do."

I got her a bottle from the fridge. She took a sip and said, "Thanks."

Then she turned her head toward the back bedroom and called out. "Bob. Here kitty, kitty."

It didn't take Bob long. He'd heard a woman calling his name and he wasn't going to pass up the chance to get petted. His head peeked out from behind the bedroom door. Devin saw him and called out again, "Come here, Bob. I've got some pets for you."

She patted her lap and Bob got the message. He trotted up from the back and we all watched as he jumped onto the couch and then settled down in Devin's lap. She smiled and began stroking his back. After a moment, she looked up at me and nodded in the direction of the dollar store.

"I met the guy online. We were in a chat room and he was posting messages about wanting to meet young girls. He said he could show them a good time. I didn't think it was right, so I decided to teach him a lesson. I would make him pay for his pervy desires.

"I started posting messages in the same chat room. It wasn't long before he took the bait and started sending me private messages. He told me he was a man's man who could teach me many things. I told him I was too young for that, but he didn't care. He got bolder and bolder, telling me how he would pleasure me. He even sent me some naked pictures.

"He kept messaging me until I agreed to meet him. Since he was expecting a young girl, I had to dress the part—a little makeup, some hair extensions and slutty clothes. That's all it took to give him his dream girl.

"We agreed to meet in the dollar store parking lot. Me on my bike, him in his red pickup. When I rode up, he honked his horn and waved me over. His first words were, 'Are you the hottie I've been dreaming of?'

"That's what I was pretending to be. His way too young hottie. He said his name was Martin, but said I should call him Marty. Big Marty. He wanted to take me to his cabin. Said we could have some drinks and get to know each other there. I told him I was too young to drink and he just smiled.

"An hour later, we ended up at his cabin. His private retreat in the woods. Only one way in, one way out. No neighbors. Perfect for what he had planned.

"The place was nicer than I expected. It looked new and was clean inside. The furniture was even new. He'd spent some money getting it all put together. The bar was well stocked and Marty made a bee line to it. He didn't bother to ask me what I wanted to drink. Instead, he made us both something he called Dew Drivers. Vodka and Mt. Dew.

"He handed me mine and said, 'Drink up.' And I did. At least I made him think I did. There was no way I was going to let Marty the pervert get me drunk in his remote cabin. After that first drink, when Marty wasn't looking I dumped mine in the fake plant at the end of the couch. He'd see my empty glass and chug his to keep up. Then he'd pour another. He kept drinking and pouring, chugging those Dew Drivers, thinking I was getting drunk with him. But I wasn't. I stayed sober and kept my wits about me.

"All the drinking finally caught up with Marty. He got sloppy drunk. Couldn't even stand up without my help. I herded him into the bedroom and pushed him down on the bed. A few minutes later, he was out cold. Snoring like a pig.

"That's when I put my plan in action. I got out my phone and took a few photos of us in compromising positions. I made sure you could see his face, but not mine.

"He was too drunk to drive me home, so I had to spend the night. The next morning, I made a big deal about us having had sex the night before and how it was my first time. Even though it never happened, he acted like he remembered the whole thing—which is exactly what I wanted him to do.

"A month later, I sent him an email telling him I was pregnant and he was the daddy. Two months after that, I dropped in on him at the bank where he worked to show him how the pregnancy was going. I started telling him I was in love and we could raise the child together. But I knew better. Old Marty had a wife and neither she nor his boss would be happy with him getting an underage girl pregnant.

"That's when he started offering me money to go away. He thought I'd leave him alone for a few hundred dollars. But he was wrong. It was going to cost him a lot more.

"That's why I went into the dollar store today, to pick up money from my pretend baby daddy."

Devin ended her story with a smile, proud of her actions. Kat was nodding her head. I wasn't sure whether she was thinking it was a good thing Devin had done or she was just happy the story was over. Bob didn't seem to care either way.

He was still in Devin's lap, purring loudly.

I wasn't sure about the story. It sounded like a lot of trouble. Months in the making. Easier to settle with one call to the police. Of course, Devin could have been making the whole thing up. Maybe there was no man and no dollar store payoff. Just a crazy girl with a crazy story.

But if it were true, it would explain why she came out of the store disguised as a pregnant teenager.

I had questions.

"When you saw this guy's messages looking for young girls, why didn't you call the police?"

Devin looked at me and shook her head slowly like I was someone from a different planet.

"What good would that do? The police in this small town don't have computer experts on staff. They deal mainly with car thieves and speeding tickets. They don't have the resources to spend weeks in a chat room hoping to catch some guy who may or may not be doing something wrong. If somebody like me didn't jump in, he'd be getting away with it."

Devin seemed upset I'd questioned her story. I knew my next question was going to upset her even more. But it was something I had to ask.

"So let me get this straight. You tricked this man into thinking you were underage. Then you made him believe he got you pregnant. Then you blackmailed him until he paid you off. And you don't see anything wrong with that?"

Devin looked at Kat, shaking her head slowly. Then she looked back at me. I could tell she was mad and working hard not to explode. She took a sip of water and said, "I wouldn't call it blackmail. The money he paid was more like a fine for doing the nasty with under-aged girls. But that's not the end of it. Earlier this morning, I sent copies of the text messages and naked photos to his wife and the local Sheriff. Won't be long before you'll be seeing the name Martin Fowler in the police log."

Kat smiled and held up her hand so Devin could high five her. I didn't join in on the hand slapping. There was something off about her story, too many things that didn't sound right. The only part I liked, assuming it was true, was the idea that the guy's wife and local police were going to get copies of the photos and text messages he had sent to Devin.

But I wasn't convinced the story was true. I didn't know Devin. I'd only just met her and in that short time she'd changed in appearance and demeanor from a young pregnant girl to a non-pregnant adult woman. For me to believe the story, I needed more details.

"So, let me ask you this. Does this guy Marty work at the dollar store? Is he still in there?"

Devin shook her head. "No, like I said before, he works at the bank. Meeting at the dollar store was my idea. A public place with lots of witnesses. Those people you saw me with earlier? They're my pretend momma and sister. They came here with me to make sure there weren't going to be any problems with Marty. And there weren't. I went in, he paid me and he left. You may have seen him come out. Short guy, stocky, red hair."

I nodded. I vaguely remembered seeing a man with red hair come out of the store. But I couldn't be sure it was the guy she was talking about. I still had questions.

"How about your pregnant belly? How'd you do that? It sure looked real to me."

She smiled. "That was easy. There's this site online that specializes in creating fake pregnant bellies that look and feel like the real thing. They're used mostly by actresses on TV or in the movies. But they'll sell to anybody.

"Their best seller is the trimester pack. Comes with three bellies so you can start with just a baby bump and then get bigger over time. That's what I bought, the three belly pack.

"If you want to see what the six month belly looks like, I've got it in my duffel bag back there. I can go get it for you."

I shook my head. "No, no need to get it out. I don't need to see it."

I wasn't surprised you could buy fake pregnant bellies online. You can find almost anything on the web these days. But I wondered how many women not on TV shows were buying pregnancy bellies and why. It was a question I wasn't going to ask. I changed the subject.

"So how do you know Kat?"

Devin smiled. "It was her dad's idea. She had just turned twenty-one and he wanted her to get some real world experience. Our clan was working Florida, so he called in a favor with one of our elders. They worked out a deal where she'd stay with us for the summer while we traveled the circuit."

"Circuit? What kind of circuit?"

Devin looked at Kat. "Is it okay if I tell him?"

She shrugged. "Might as well. He'll find out soon enough anyway."

Chapter Seven

"The locals call us 'Travelers'. It isn't a name we like but one that we got stuck with. Our clan's home base is in Ohio but we spend our winters in Florida. We come down with our trucks and trailers and set up camp outside of small towns. The men go into town and go door to door offering to do roof repairs and driveway resealing.

"The clan would buy blank canvases and the women would stay in camp and paint Florida landscape scenes on them. They'd sign the paintings with names like Harold Newton and Al Black and other well-known highway men painters.

"When Kat joined us, she was partnered up with me. My job was to go out and try to sell the paintings to tourists. Kat and I would set up on the side of the road, put the paintings on display and price them for fifty bucks each. Tourists would stop, see the signatures and think they were getting a bargain. We never claimed the paintings were authentic. We just played dumb and took their money."

Devin smiled and pointed at Kat. "This one was a quick learner. She could sense when a customer was interested in a particular painting. She'd tell them the paintings couldn't be real, that they had to be fakes. But for some reason, that would make them want the paintings even more. They'd end up buying two or three and were always happy to do it, thinking they were taking advantage of us dumb girls.

"Eventually word would get around that the paintings

were fake and the sheriff would run us off. We'd lay low for a few days and then set up again further down the road.

"We were so good at this that our clan elders decided to give us a chance to sell something with a lot more profit potential. They called it 'trailer picking'. Basically, we'd go out and look for camping trailers we could buy.

"The sellers were almost always men and when they heard the sob story Kat and I would tell them about how we needed a place to live but couldn't afford much, they'd drop their prices and sell us their trailers real cheap. A few even gave us their trailers for free.

"We'd haul the trailer back to camp and our men folk would slap on a coat of paint and spray undercoating to hide any rust. Then we run ads and sell the trailers for a big profit.

"The only problem was we'd have to keep moving camp every few weeks to hide from buyers who came looking for a refund."

Devin paused and looked at Kat to see if she wanted to add anything. Kat just shook her head. I didn't know whether she didn't have anything to add or she felt bad about some of the things they'd done. Either way, I decided it might be a good time to ask a few questions.

"These Travelers, are they the same as gypsies?"

Devin shook her head. "No. Travelers are definitely not the same as Gypsies. Don't ever call a Traveler a Gypsy unless you want to get your head knocked off. Travelers are Irish and we don't associate with Gypsies."

That was news to me. "So you and Kat traveled with a clan, camping out in Florida and running scams on the locals? Do you feel bad about that? About ripping people off?"

Devin's eyes flashed with anger. "We didn't rip anyone off.

In fact, most of the people who bought from us thought they were taking advantage of us. They thought they were getting away with something. We never pressured them. Buying from us was always their choice. Same when people were selling us their trailers. It was always their choice to sell or not."

She took a sip of water and continued. "Our men folk worked hard and did decent roofing jobs at reasonable prices. Most of their customers were happy with what they got. The few that weren't—well, you can't please everyone."

Devin looked at Kat and shook her head. "I'm not too sure about your friend here. He seems to believe I'm some kind of con artist or crook. You want to set him straight?"

Devin crossed her arms and stared at me, anger flashing in her eyes.

Kat saw what was happening and tried to calm her down. "Devin, he's just asking questions. The same kind I'd be asking if I'd just met you and heard the stories you've been telling. You got to admit, when you tell him about wearing a fake pregnant belly to get money from a man it could make him wonder about you."

Devin nodded. "Maybe. But I don't like it when people think I'm a con artist."

I decided it was time to try to smooth things over. I smiled at Devin and said, "Sorry if I offended you. I didn't mean to. It's just that your stories are so interesting, especially about living with Travelers. I've heard about them, but never from someone who actually worked with them. I'd like to hear more, especially about your and Kat's adventures."

Devin had cooled down a little but wasn't smiling. She looked at Kat. "Is this guy okay? He's not the law is he?"

Kat laughed and raised her thumb in my direction. "Him, the law? You've got to be kidding. If you knew what he did for my father in Key West, you wouldn't be asking that question. He might not be a Traveler but he's definitely one of us."

I didn't know whether to take that as a compliment or not. I always considered myself a law abiding citizen, someone who stuck to the straight and narrow. At least, that was the life I'd lived before I came to Florida. Things had changed since then.

Kat's words seemed to calm Devin. She forced a smile in my direction. "I trust Kat. You I don't know and I won't trust until I have a reason to."

I understood. Trust is something you earn. But since I didn't expect to be spending much time with Devin, I was pretty sure I wouldn't need to earn her trust.

I was wrong.

Chapter Eight

We were still in the motorhome sitting in the dollar store parking lot. Devin was telling me how she and Kat had met and how they'd worked the Traveler circuit together.

"So don't leave me hanging. What happened with your trailer picking. . ."

I started to say 'scam' but thought better of it considering how Devin had reacted earlier. So I said, "... trailer picking business. How'd that work out?"

Devin glanced over at Kat, a look that asked, "Can I tell him?"

Kat nodded slightly. "Yeah, you can tell him. Just don't mention the Trailer Monkeys."

I couldn't let that pass. "Trailer monkeys? You can't bring up something like that and not tell me about it. So either we end it here or I get to hear about the Trailer Monkeys."

Devin looked at Kat again. She was trying to hold back a smile, but couldn't. Kat looked at her, saw the smile and shook her head. Devin sort of giggled and Kat gave in. "Okay, you can tell him about the Trailer Monkeys. But tell the other part first. And don't forget to mention the truck."

Devin smiled. "You sure you don't want to tell the story? Because if you do, go right ahead."

"No, you tell it. But before you start, would you like something to drink? There's some Mountain Dew, more water and a bottle of wine in the fridge."

Devin smiled. "Let's save the wine for later. Right now, water would be good."

I got up and got each of us a bottle of cold water then settled back in my chair, ready to listen to whatever story she might tell.

She took a sip of water and started in.

"The elders gave us a truck so we could haul trailers we brought back to camp with us. The truck wasn't new. In fact, it was pretty old and showed the scars of being used for years to haul roofing pitch and blacktop sealer. But it had a trailer hitch and a radio, and that's pretty much all we needed.

"It was dark blue, or had been when it was new. The sun had faded it to more of a chalky pastel blue. You didn't want to lean against it, 'cause if you did, you'd come away with some of that blue on you.

"After washing it and cleaning up the inside that truck became our daily ride. We called it 'Old Blue'.

"We'd start each day heading out on back roads, looking for camping trailers parked in back yards. When we'd see one, we'd stop, introduce ourselves and ask if the trailer was for sale.

"Most of the time, the people we talked to were friendly. They were happy to see us and would often invite us in for iced tea or cold water. More often than not, though, they weren't interested in selling their trailer. But they almost always knew someone who had a trailer for sale, and they'd send us over to talk to them.

"When we found one for sale, we'd inspect it, looking for serious problems like water leaks in the roof, rat infestations or rusted frames. Those were the kinds of problems we couldn't fix and we'd pass on those deals.

"But usually, at least once a week, we'd find a trailer in

good shape that we could get a good deal on and we'd buy it. We'd pay with cash, get the title and hitch it up to Old Blue and haul it back to camp.

"The men there would work on the outside to make it presentable while the women would pretty up the inside. They'd sew new curtains, spray good smelling stuff and make it nice and clean.

"When the trailer was ready, we'd hook it up to Old Blue and take it into town and park it near one of the livestock barns or in a shopping center parking lot. We'd put a 'for sale' sign on it, pull out our folding chairs and sit out front, waving as cars went by.

"Saturdays were the best days and usually within three or four hours we'd find a buyer willing to pay our price. We'd collect the money, give him the title, and drive Old Blue back to camp.

"The clan would let us keep about five hundred dollars of whatever profit we made on the sale. The rest of the money went into the general fund, which the elders controlled.

"Kat and I bought and sold eleven trailers that first season. We were both flush with money when the clan started packing up at the end of winter to head back up north.

"That's when the trouble started."

Chapter Nine

Devin had opened up about how she'd met Kat, but she hadn't gotten to the part about the Trailer Monkeys. And really that's all what I wanted to hear. So even though it was getting late in the day, I didn't stop her.

"Like I said earlier, our clan was based in Ohio and at the end of the season, we'd pack up all the trucks and head back up north. The families had been doing this for as long as I could remember. They worked Florida in the winter, and went back up north during the summer."

"When word spread through the camp that it was time to start packing for Ohio, I wasn't happy. Kat and I were doing pretty good buying and selling trailers and I wasn't ready to give it up. I'd grown to like Florida and wanted to stay.

"I talked with Kat and we agreed that, if I stayed in Florida, we could keep doing what we were doing. With what we had saved up, we could afford to find a place to rent and have money left over to buy trailers we could sell. When I broke the news to the clan that I wouldn't be going back to Ohio with them, the elders didn't take it well.

"They said I would be breaking a family tradition and, to make matters worse, would probably be meeting and socializing with men not in the clan.

"They didn't like the idea of me staying behind, but since I was of legal age and they had no control over Kat, there wasn't anything they could do about it. But as punishment they wanted me to pay a 'staying behind' fee to cover my share of camp expenses. I'd already given them 70% of the profit we made and I wasn't giving them any more.

"My father took my side on this. He's pretty high up in the clan and when he spoke, others listened. They knew if they wanted to stay on his good side, they wouldn't go against him. And they didn't.

"We ended up buying Old Blue. Probably paid more for the old truck than it was worth, but we needed transportation and Old Blue was available."

Devin continued with her story for another half hour, going into great detail about the first few months she and Kat had spent together. She talked about the little apartment they rented and how they furnished it with things they bought at second hand stores. She talked about their neighbors and the landlord's lack of hair on his head and all the hair on his back. She talked about the color of the walls in the bathroom and having to use sheets to cover the windows. She went on and on and on going into great detail about things I really didn't care about.

Kat seemed to enjoy listening to Devin reminiscing about old times but it wasn't doing anything for me. Or Bob. He had given up about an hour in and gone to his spot in the back.

Mercifully, she finally stopped talking. She'd been going on nonstop and needed another bottle of water. I knew she wasn't finished though, because she hadn't gotten to the part about the Trailer Monkeys. But I was afraid if I encouraged her to continue, she would go on for another hour or two.

The funny thing was she didn't seem like the kind of person who liked to talk. It was almost like she was trying to run out the clock, to keep us in the dollar store parking lot as long as she could.

It was time for me to step in and close her down.

I pointed to the clock above the kitchen sink. "Devin, I hate to interrupt you and I do want to hear the rest of the story but not today. Kat and I have another hundred miles to go before we get to our campsite and we need to get there before the rangers close the gates.

"Kat said you had a package for her father. You have it with you?"

She shook her head. "No, I don't. It's not the kind of thing you carry with you in public. It's back at my place. We'll have to go there to get it."

That was okay with me. We could take her there, pick up the package and be gone. "Is your place close? Is it here in Crystal River?"

"No, it's in Niceville."

"Niceville? Is that a trailer park or something?"

She shook her head. "No, Niceville's not a trailer park. It's a city in Florida. That's where I live. That's where we need to go to pick up the package."

I nodded. "Okay, we'll go there. How far is it?"

I was expecting her to say it was maybe ten, twenty miles down the road. Some place close. Some place we could get to quickly, pick up the package and drive on to our campsite before dark. But I was wrong.

Devin stood up and stretched. "Niceville is up by Panama City. About seven hours from here. If we leave now, we might be able to get there by midnight. But I don't think it's a road you want to drive on after dark, especially in a motorhome."

I didn't like the direction this was going. "Are you kidding

41

me? You live seven hours from here? And I'm going to have to take you there to pick up the package? And there's no way we're going to make it there tonight?"

She smiled. "That's pretty much it."

I thought about it for a moment then had two more questions. I hoped the answer to the first was 'yes' and the second was 'no'.

"Do you have a car and want us to follow you there?"

She shook her head. "No, I don't have a car. Not here. It's in Niceville. I'm going to have to ride with you."

I struck out on the first question and was pretty sure I was going to strike out on the second.

"Where do you plan to sleep tonight?"

She looked around, first at Kat then at me then down the hallway to my bedroom and then back at the couch. She smiled and said, "I hope I can sleep in here with you two. Looks like you've got plenty of room. But if that's a problem, I can go back into the dollar store and buy a tent."

I looked at Kat and she smiled, I knew what she was thinking. She wanted me to let Devin spend the night in the motorhome with us. As far as she was concerned, it was the only sensible option. Not me though, I could think of several others. I could put Devin on a bus to Niceville. We could meet her there. Or I could put her in a cheap motel for the night. Or we could buy that tent she was talking about. But I didn't figure Kat would be happy with any of those ideas, so I relented.

"Devin, no need for a tent. You can stay in here with us. We'll just have to figure out where everyone is going to sleep."

My motorhome is not like the big ones the rich and

famous drive. At just twenty-seven feet long, mine's about half the size of those. It still has all the conveniences of home, including a small kitchen and a bathroom and shower, but it only has one bedroom, and it's in the back. It's the ideal size for one or two people traveling together.

But there's a problem when you have guests staying over. With only one bathroom and only one real bed, it means the guest has to sleep on the fold out couch. It's not particularly comfortable but it does make into a bed.

The plan when we left that morning was I would be sleeping in the bed and Kat would sleep on the couch. It was her idea, and if that was what she wanted, that's what we would be doing.

In a perfect world, Kat and I would be more than just friends and this trip would have been a romantic getaway. We'd be sharing my bed. But it's not a perfect world; we were just friends and we'd be sleeping alone. But adding Devin would change that, at least for one of us.

Kat and I had known each other for a little over a month and out of necessity we'd spent a lot of time together. We ate most of our meals together, watched TV and movies together and even did our laundry together. But we hadn't slept together. Not because I didn't find her attractive because, believe me, I did, but mainly because I knew who her father was and his last words to me when I was leaving Key West with her were, "Keep her safe, don't get her mad, and don't fool around with her. Got it?"

I got it. Her father was not someone you disobeyed. Most of those who did didn't live to tell about it.

Chapter Ten

When it became clear that we would be taking Devin to Niceville, it also became clear we shouldn't be wasting any more time sitting in the dollar store parking lot. The sooner we got back on the road the sooner we'd get to Niceville and the sooner we'd be rid of Devin. I let the girls know we were leaving.

I got up and made sure all the doors were locked and everything was stowed away. I checked on Bob in the back and after seeing he was okay, I came back up front expecting to get in the driver's seat.

Neither Devin nor Kat had moved from the couch. As I walked by, Kat reached out, took my hand and pulled me toward her. She said, "Walker, I want you sit here by me for a minute. There's something I want to talk about."

I didn't want to sit. I wanted to drive. I'd been sitting for the last two hours listening to Devin talk and that was plenty of sitting and listening for me. I didn't say that out loud though. Instead, like a good boy, I sat down on the couch beside Kat. No point getting her mad.

Still holding my hand, she said, "Devin and I were thinking that, instead of camping at Manatee Springs tonight, we should drive on to Perry and spend the night there. That'll give us a good starting point in the morning. It'll make it easier for us to get to Niceville during the day."

She let go of my hand and reached across me to get the

Florida atlas I kept in the driver's back seat pocket. She flipped to the page showing Florida's west coast. "See, if we stay on 98, it'll take us all the way to Perry. They have a Walmart Super Center there where we can get food and gas. From there, we can head over to Rocky's campground. It's just a few miles out of town. If we leave now, we'll get there before dark."

I looked at the map then back at Kat. "What about the reservations you made for us at Manatee Springs? Why don't we just stay there?"

She looked over at Devin and then back at me. "Walker, I didn't really make reservations for us at Manatee Springs. I knew we'd be picking Devin up and I knew we needed to take her to Niceville. I figured when you found out, you'd want to drive as far as you could today so we'd be able to get to Niceville tomorrow. I'm right about that, aren't I?"

She was. I reluctantly nodded in agreement.

She smiled and patted me on the knee. "Good. Let's forget about Manatee Springs. We can stop there on the way back if you want. But right now we need to go another hundred and fifty miles before we set up camp. You ready to drive?"

I was.

I stood. "If either of you need to use the facilities, now's the time."

Kat raised her hand and said, "Me first." Then she headed to the bathroom in the back.

I checked again to make the sure the side door was locked then headed up front and settled into the driver's seat. I was surprised when Devin sat in the passenger seat beside me.

She looked over and whispered, "Walker, I don't know how well you know Kat, but let me give you some advice.

Don't trust her. And don't believe everything she says. She's famous for being the queen of the long con."

From behind us we heard the bathroom door unlock. Devin got up and quickly moved back to the couch. She was sitting there when Kat rejoined us.

Devin stood and said, "My turn," and then headed back to the bathroom.

As soon as she had closed the door behind her, Kat came up and sat in the passenger seat just as Devin had done. She leaned over and whispered. "Be careful around Devin. She's the queen of the long con. Don't trust her."

From behind us, we could hear the sound of water running in the bathroom sink. Devin was washing her hands and would soon be out. Kat stood and moved to the couch. She was sitting there when Devin came out, acting like she hadn't moved an inch.

With both girls on the couch, I pointed to the empty passenger seat beside me. "Either one of you want to ride shotgun?"

Devin looked at Kat and whispered something. I couldn't tell what she said but it made Kat smile. Then Kat said, "Unless you need one of us up there, we'd like to stay back here and talk. Would that be okay?"

I was thinking, *Yeah, that'd be great. Both of you stay back there. I'll drive.* I actually preferred it that way. Most of the time when I traveled, it was just me and Bob. We liked it that way. I didn't tell the girls this, instead I just said, "Well, we're leaving then. Buckle up."

I started the motorhome and pulled to the edge of the dollar store parking lot. When traffic cleared, I pulled out onto US 98 and headed north toward Perry.

Behind me, the two women who had each told me not to trust the other sat on the couch whispering. No doubt working out details of the long con, which I was apparently already part of.

Chapter Eleven

As I drove north, unable to make out what Kat and Devin were whispering about behind me, I couldn't help but think of what Warren Buffet had once said about playing poker. "If you've been in the game 30 minutes and don't know who the patsy is, it's you."

We weren't playing poker, but Kat and Devin had some kind of game going and I was pretty sure I was the patsy.

Problem was I didn't know what kind of game we were playing. I didn't know what the rules were or what was at stake. All I knew for sure was somehow me and my motorhome were involved.

The passenger seat beside me didn't stay empty for long. Bob trotted up from the back and hopped up on it. He sat facing me and when he caught my eye, he huffed out a grunt. He was asking, "What have you gotten us into this time?"

Bob had been with me when we'd had guests before—almost always women and almost always starting out as a favor for a friend. The friend would say, "It's an easy trip. Just take her there in your motorhome and when she gets done with whatever she needs to do, bring her back. Easy peasy."

Except it rarely worked out that way. Almost always what should have been an easy trip turned into something not so easy that lasted several days longer than planned. Usually strangers would join us along the way and the mission would evolve into something bigger with me playing the leading role.

Bob didn't mind it when strangers slept on the couch during these trips as long as they were cat friendly and let him snuggle up beside them during the night.

I looked over at him and he mouthed out a soft meow, kind of like he was saying, "Good luck." Then he settled down in the seat and began licking his paws. He paid particular attention to his claws. He wanted them to be ready for whatever lay ahead.

It'd been almost an hour since we left Crystal River. The road we were on, US 98, was a well maintained four lane blacktop that cut through the dense pine forests of Florida's Nature Coast. Traffic had been light and we were making good time. The road had once been the main road into Florida and back then it had been filled with small motels and roadside attractions, kind of like Route 66.

Driving this road in the old days was like cruising through a two hundred mile long county fair, interesting and somewhat outlandish attractions along the way vying for your attention. But that ended when Interstate 75 was built. Most of the northern tourists chose high speed travel on the super highway rather than the slow scenic route we were taking today.

With tourist traffic all but gone, most of the business that depended on the daily stream of visitors saw their revenues dry up and eventually had to close. The empty block shells of these long forgotten attractions were now being taken over by Mother Nature. Covered with vines and littered with the forgotten memories of long ago travelers.

A few small towns had somehow survived, including Chiefland, the town we were about to enter. A large Marathon gas station with several log trucks in the parking lot marked the town's entrance. The gas pumps reminded me to check our fuel situation. The gas gauge showed a little under half a tank, more than enough to get us to Perry but not much further. I'd definitely want to fill up there before we set up camp for the night.

Leaving Chiefland behind, I brought the motorhome back up to cruising speed, just above the posted speed limit of fifty-five. I stayed in the right lane, making sure any cars coming up from behind could pass without a problem. The reality was there wasn't much traffic to worry about and the silky smooth recently repaved blacktop made driving it in a motorhome a real pleasure.

A tap on my shoulder got my attention. Devin had gotten up off the couch and made her way up front. Bracing herself against the ceiling with one hand to keep her balance in the moving motorhome, she pointed to the passenger seat where Bob had curled up into a tight ball and was sleeping.

"Kat went back to the bedroom to make a phone call. She said she might stay there and take a nap. Mind if I sit up here with you?"

I didn't mind. I thought it might be interesting to hear what she had to say with Kat out of the way.

I pointed to Bob. "If he'll move, feel free to sit there."

She reached down and lightly touched the fur on his back. He opened one sleepy eye and raised his head just enough to see Devin standing there. He yawned, let out a short meow and scooted over, giving her enough room to sit.

She sat in the seat beside him, being careful not to push him off the edge into the wheel well by the door. Bob sensed she was being careful and he rewarded her by moving into her lap and letting her pet his head.

A few minutes after this, Devin pointed out the

51

windshield. "You need to slow down. We're coming up on Fanning Springs and there's a speed trap there. They'll have a cop set up behind the speed limit sign at the city limits and another on the downhill side of the bridge going out of town.

"They'll write you a ticket even if you're just a mile over. You'll want to start slowing down now and keep it below the limit all the way through town."

I could see the city limit sign up on the right with the reduced speed sign just beyond. The posted limit was fifty-five and I was doing just over that. The new limit was forty-five. I didn't want a ticket, so I slowed to forty.

That didn't satisfy Devin. "You're still going too fast. The next sign is going to be thirty-five. Get your speed down now."

There was a long stretch of blacktop ahead and I couldn't see any new speed signs but Devin acted like she knew this stretch of road, so I took my foot off the gas and let the motorhome burn off some speed. I had just gotten it under thirty when I saw the police cruiser with the radar gun aimed in our direction. It was hiding behind a large roadside sign advertising the El Dorado motel and restaurant.

Devin looked over at me. "I told you he'd be there. There'll be another one up ahead. Keep it slow until we get past him."

Three miles ahead, on the downhill side of the Suwanee River Bridge, a place where cars would naturally pick up speed, sat another cruiser with its radar gun pointed at us.

This time, Devin didn't say anything. She didn't need to. She'd been right about the cruiser. She pointed at the cop and waved. He didn't wave back.

When we were well past him, she said, "Cross City is

next. It's about ten miles ahead. You can run forty-five until we get there. But you'll want to slow down to thirty-five when we get into town."

I was glad she was telling me this. I didn't want to get a speeding ticket in a small town in Florida.

"So I guess you know this area pretty well?" I asked.

"Yeah, I do. I drive through here a lot."

"For your job?"

"Sometimes. But mostly my work is on the other side of the state. I come through here when I visit friends down in Crystal River."

I wanted to know more so I kept asking questions.

"What kind of work do you do?"

She didn't answer right away. I had a feeling she was trying to come up with something that wouldn't reveal too much about her. Something that would fit in with whatever game or con she and Kat were running. Finally, she said, "I'm a collector. Freelance. What about you? What do you do for a living?"

I wasn't going to answer her question, at least not until she gave me a better answer to the question I'd asked her. "So you're a collector? What do you collect? Art? Antiques? Cars?"

She smiled. "I collect different things for different people. Sometimes art. Sometimes money. But mostly paper."

"Paper? What kind of paper?"

She smiled again. "The kind people pay me to collect for them. Deeds, legal documents, warrants and sometimes titles. What about you, what do you do for a living?"

Kat had told me not to trust Devin and so far I hadn't seen any reason why I should. I didn't want to tell her that thanks to a legal settlement I had enough money stashed away so I didn't need to work. But I had to tell her something. Since Kat had probably told her a little about the work I'd done for her father, I decided to go with that.

"I work with computers—whenever I can find someone to hire me. Lately, it's been slim pickings."

Devin nodded and I was surprised she didn't ask a follow up question about my work. Most people do. Instead, she asked, "You live in this motorhome full time?"

She'd asked me this before, disguised as a pregnant teen just a few hours earlier. I gave her the same answer I gave then.

"Yeah, I live in here full time. Just me and Mango Bob."

He lifted his head when he heard me say his name. He breathed out a soft meow, letting me know he was close. I liked that about him.

Devin stroked his back and he started purring. "How'd he get the Mango part of his name?"

I'd been asked this before and didn't feel like retelling the whole story, so I just said, "The girl who rescued him named him. She found him as starving kitten on Mango Street in Englewood and decided the street should be part of his name."

Devin nodded. "I like it. Mango Street. Maybe that's where the Mango Blues come from."

I'd never heard of Mango Blues and had no idea what she was talking about. "Mango Blues? Is that a song?"

"Yeah it's a song. From a guy named Floyd Lloyd. You sure you've never heard it, Mango Blues?"

I was pretty sure I'd never heard of it. I think I would have remembered a song that shared the name of my cat in the title. I didn't tell her that though. I just said, "No, never heard it."

"Well, you should listen to it. You might like it. Maybe Bob will like it too. It's an easy title to remember, Mango Blues."

I nodded. "I won't forget. Mango Blues."

There wasn't much I could add to the subject, so I didn't say anything else. A few minutes later, Devin pointed over her shoulder and asked, "How long you been living like this?"

Answering questions was one of the downsides of traveling with strangers. Still, it helped kill time, so I played nice.

"About a year."

"You have a wife? Any kids?"

I laughed. "I have an ex-wife, no kids. How about you? You have a husband?"

"Not anymore."

"Divorce?"

"No, not a divorce. He died. I shot him."

Her answer took me by surprise. I didn't know what to say next. But I felt I had to say something, so I asked, "What kind of gun did you use?"

Upon hearing this, she burst out laughing.

Chapter Twelve

"Did you just ask me what kind of gun I used when I shot my husband? That's your question? You're not asking why I shot him? You just want to know what caliber I used?"

I smiled. "Look, I don't meet many women who tell me they've shot their husbands so I don't have a lot of experience in these situations. Asking you about the gun was the only thing I could think of. That and, 'How many shots did it take to kill him?'"

She laughed. "Walker, I'm starting to like you."

I nodded then repeated my question. "So what kind of gun did you use? Seriously, what was it? A pistol? A rifle? Shotgun?"

She looked at me, shaking her head, offended that I'd ask such a question. But then she smiled and said, "I didn't shoot anyone. I just said that so you'd quit asking questions about my personal life. Usually when I tell a man I shot my husband, they quit asking questions. Not you though. You wanted to know more. That usually means you're either a cop or some kind of investigator. Is that what you are? A cop? Because if you are, you have to tell me. It's the law."

I was pretty sure she was wrong about that. Cops don't have to tell you they're cops. They don't have to tell you anything. All they have to do is read you your rights when they arrest you.

I didn't tell her that. Instead I told her the truth. "I'm not a cop. Never been one. Don't plan to be one in the future. I respect what they do and I'm happy they're around when you need one. But I couldn't do the kind of work they do. The hours are too long, the risks are too high and the pay is too low. It's not for me."

My answer seemed to satisfy her. But not Bob. He'd heard enough talk. It was disturbing his sleep, so he jumped down out of Devin's lap and headed to the back bedroom. Probably to nap up with Kat.

With Bob gone, Devin kicked off her sandals and put her bare feet up on the dash. Her tan legs were hard to miss. She caught me looking and said, "I just had them waxed. They're real smooth. You want to feel?"

Had I not been driving a motorhome down the highway, my answer would have probably been 'yes'. But sadly, even though I was tempted, I wasn't going to let her newly waxed tan legs distract me.

"I appreciate the offer, but right now I'll have to pass. Maybe later."

She laughed. "It was a limited time offer. Don't expect me to repeat it, especially when Kat's around."

I'd almost forgotten Kat was with us. I checked the rear view mirror to see if she had come up from the back, but she hadn't.

Devin laughed. "I see what you're doing. You're checking to make sure Kat didn't hear you flirt with me. That would create problems, wouldn't it?"

I didn't answer. I just kept driving.

Devin wouldn't let it go. "So you think Kat would like it if she knew you were flirting with me? Think I should go tell her?"

I didn't know whether she was teasing or was serious. Either way, it didn't matter. Kat and I were just friends and just barely that. We'd known each other less than a month, kissed just once and never shared a bed.

I didn't know what Kat had told Devin about me but I was pretty sure she wouldn't have said we were in any kind of relationship. But then again, I'm usually wrong when it comes to figuring out how women feel about me. So I just said, "I wasn't trying to flirt with you, but if you took it that way and think Kat should know about it, go ahead and tell her. See what she says."

Chapter Thirteen

Devin didn't budge from her seat. She didn't go back and tell Kat anything. She just sat there, staring at the road ahead. Not saying anything. This was fine with me.

Glancing over at the GPS, it looked like we'd be in Perry in about a half hour. I could easily go that long without conversation. Hopefully, Devin could do the same.

But it wasn't to be. Five minutes after she'd last spoke, she turned to me and asked, "Do you think I'm pretty?"

It was a question she already knew the answer to. Every guy who saw her knew she was not only 'pretty' but a real knockout. No doubt she'd been told how pretty she was all her life. But I wasn't going to get sucked into her web by giving her the answer she wanted. So I said, "I haven't really thought about it. How about you? Do you think you're pretty?"

I'd turned the tables on her with my question. Her answer, if she gave one, would tell me a lot about her.

"It really doesn't matter what I think. What I want to know is what you think. Do you think I'm pretty?"

I looked over at her and she smiled, eager to hear my answer. The one I gave probably wasn't the one she expected. I said, "You know that pretty actress on the TV show where they hunt down zombies? The girl with blonde hair and the great body?"

Devin nodded. "Yeah I know who you're talking about."

"Good. Well, without a doubt, I think you're prettier than any of the zombies on that show."

I tried not to laugh when I gave my answer. I just kept looking ahead, my eyes on the road. I knew if I looked over at her, I wouldn't be able to keep a straight face.

Almost a minute went by before she said anything. Then, "So you think I'm prettier than a zombie. I guess I'll take that as a compliment. But maybe when you're not driving, you'll be able to get a closer look at me. Maybe tonight, after Kat goes to bed."

I looked over and she winked. I shook my head and focused on the road. I didn't know how to respond to Devin's offer to get a closer look when Kat wasn't around. I hoped she was just kidding but I wasn't sure.

It was then that Kat came up front to join us. She sat on the couch directly behind me and put her hand on my shoulder. "Devin hasn't been up here bothering you, has she?"

I looked over at Devin. She was doing her best to look innocent, almost angelic. Trying to hide the hard time she'd been giving me. I decided to play along.

"No, she's hasn't been bothering me. In fact, she helped me avoid a speeding ticket back there in Fanning Springs. But then again, for the last fifty miles I've had to look at her big bare feet up on my dash."

Kat laughed. "She didn't try to seduce you, did she?"

I shook my head. "If she did, I didn't notice it. All I saw were her big feet."

Devin reached over and punched me on the arm. "If you didn't want my feet up on the dash, you should have told me to move them."

I rubbed my arm in mock pain. "Don't punch me while I'm driving. You could cause a wreck that way. And yes, I'm tired of looking at your feet. Get them off the dash. And when we stop, get a paper towel from the kitchen and wipe the dash down. I don't want it to smell like feet the rest of the trip."

Devin took her feet off the dash, put her sandals back on and crossed her arms. When I looked over at her, she stuck her tongue out. And winked.

Kat didn't see the wink, or if she did, she didn't say anything about it. She just pointed out the windshield and said, "Perry's just up ahead. Walmart's on the other side of town, so stay on 98 all the way through. When you get to the red light by KFC, take a right into the Walmart parking lot."

I nodded and drove on, looking forward to taking a break at Walmart while trying not to think about the meaning of Devin's wink.

Chapter Fourteen

Getting through the small town of Perry was easy. Four lane most of the way. A couple of stop lights and not much traffic. When we reached the light at the KFC, I took a right and pulled into the Walmart lot.

Three motorhomes were parked on the far right side of the lot, probably planning to stay the night. We could have done the same but Kat had a different plan. She wanted to pick up supplies and drive on.

I pulled into an empty space close to the Murphy gas station at the front of the lot and parked. I turned to Kat who was still sitting on the couch behind me.

"We're here. What's the plan?"

She stood, stretched and said, "While you were up here flirting with Devin, I checked your fridge to see what kind of food you had. I didn't find much. So my plan is to go into Walmart, get a roasted chicken, a Caesar salad, a couple bottles of wine and maybe something for breakfast. You coming with?"

I shook my head. "No. I'm staying out here. While you're in there, I'll pull over to the Murphy station and top off our tank. I want to be sure we have plenty of gas before we head out in the morning."

Kat nodded and looked at Devin. "How about you? You staying out here with him or going in with me?"

Devin looked over at me and said, "I'm not staying out

here with him. He's been mean to me. Saying bad things about my feet. I'm going with you."

Devin went out first and Kat started to follow. Then she stopped and said, "Walker, you better be here when we come back. Don't get any ideas about leaving without us. Understood?"

I nodded. "Don't worry. I'll be here."

I watched as the two girls walked across the lot heading toward the store's main entrance. About halfway there, Devin turned and looked back at me and smiled. Almost as quickly, she turned away.

When I was sure they were both inside the store, I went back to my bedroom. Kat had been in there for a long time while I was driving. She was presumably taking a nap. But if she wasn't, she had plenty of time to search the room looking for secret compartments.

The bed in my motorhome is built on a platform. The mattress can be raised to reach a large storage area underneath. I hadn't shown this to Kat, but it was a common feature in trailers as well as motorhomes, and since she had a lot of experience with trailers from her picking days, she might wonder what I had stored below mine.

Usually people keep heavy coats, extra blankets, and things that are too large for the closet in the under-bed storage area. I do the same, but I also have a lock-box filled with important papers, my pistol, several thousand dollars in cash and a roll of gold coins. The box is bolted to the floor, and I keep it covered with an old rug to keep it hidden.

I usually leave the key in the lock—except when I know I'll be away from the motorhome for an extended period of time. Since I hadn't planned to be away, the key was still in the unlocked box. At least, it was supposed to be.

Because I was traveling with the 'queens of the long con', I thought it might be wise to check that the box was undisturbed.

I lifted the top of the bed platform and locked it in the up position so the mattress wouldn't come down and bang me on the head. I moved the extra blankets and heavy coat out of the way so I could get to the rug that was covering the lock box. Moving the rug away, it looked like the box was undisturbed. I could have left it at that but decided I'd better check the contents.

I unlocked the box and lifted the top. Inside, I could see my passport and other documents were exactly where I'd left them. The thick envelope filled with cash was still sealed. Untouched.

But the roll of gold coins had been moved. Instead of standing vertically, the roll was now on its side with the top slightly ajar. It was possible, even likely, the roll had tipped over on its own when the motorhome leaned to one side as we pulled in or out of a parking lot. That kind of thing happens a lot.

But it still bothered me to find the tube of gold coins lying on its side. The small plastic tube didn't look like much, but based on the current price of gold, the twenty US Eagle gold coins in it were worth close to thirty thousand dollars. I had nineteen more rolls just like it safely stored in my bank deposit box. This one roll was my 'just in case' fund while on the road. I hoped I never needed it but if I did, it would be easy to convert to cash.

I picked up the roll and shook it. If it rattled, it meant at least one coin was missing. But there was no rattle. The coins were tightly packed, the same way they'd always been.

I tightened the top and put the roll back in the lock box.

To keep it from moving around, I shoved the heavy box of 357 shells I keep for my pistol up against it. I arranged the documents inside to hide the shells and then I closed the top. I locked the box and put the key in my pocket. Then I put everything back the way it was and lowered the bed back into its sleeping position.

Satisfied that Kat had not gotten into the lock box, I went back up front, started the motorhome and pulled it over to the fuel lane at the Murphy station. It took almost fifty gallons to top off the tank. Pretty much what I expected. At ten miles a gallon, the motorhome wasn't what you would call fuel efficient but if I wanted fuel efficiency I'd be driving a Prius.

The advantage of a motorhome over a Prius was the motorhome had a bathroom, a shower, a kitchen and bedroom, none of which the Prius had.

After filling the tanks, I pulled back into parking space where the girls had gotten out. I killed the engine and waited for their return.

While waiting, I went back and checked on Bob's food and water. He was pretty particular about how much food he wanted in his bowl. When it didn't meet his requirements, he'd let me know. He'd come up and meow constantly until I followed back to his bowl. Then he'd nudge it with his nose, as if to say, "You'd need to take care of this."

And, of course, I always would.

It'd been a while since I last saw Bob so I decided it might be a good idea to check on him. I knew he wasn't in the bedroom, I would have seen him there when I checked under the bed. He wasn't in the bathroom either. That meant he was probably in one of his favorite hidey holes. He has several, including one behind the couch.

I looked there first and that's where he was—sleeping. I didn't want to bother him so I left him alone and returned to the driver's seat to watch for the girls' return.

It was a long wait.

Chapter Fifteen

Kat and Devin said they weren't going to spend much time in Walmart. They were going to go in, get some food and be right back out. Shouldn't have taken more than ten minutes. But they'd been gone for almost thirty minutes and I was starting to wonder if they were coming back.

We still had miles to go before we set up camp for the night and I didn't want to waste time sitting in the Walmart parking lot. I pulled out my phone and punched in Kat's number. I figured I'd call her and ask what was going on.

Ten seconds after I dialed, I heard the beginning strains of Aerosmith's "Janie's Got a Gun", the ring tone of Kat's phone. It was coming from inside the motorhome. I got up and followed Steven Tyler's voice to her phone, which was lying on the couch. It had probably slipped out of her pocket there earlier.

No phone meant no way to call Kat. My other option was to call Devin. But having just met her a few hours earlier, and never having received a call from her, I didn't have her number. But Kat did. I figured it might be on her phone.

I picked up the phone Kat had left behind and pressed the home button, only to discover it was password protected. Without the password I couldn't log in and couldn't get Devin's number. That meant I wouldn't be calling either of them.

I sat back in the driver's seat and watched the customers

going in and out of Walmart, hoping Kat and Devin would soon make an appearance.

A few minutes later, I heard sirens in the distance. They got louder and louder until two police cruisers with blue lights flashing pulled into Walmart parking lot and stopped at the store's main entrance.

Just behind them was an EMT van. Two EMTs from the van got out, retrieved a stretcher and wheeled it into the store. Customers were leaving the store en masse, some in a panic. A few came out slowly, looking over their shoulders trying to see what was going on inside. I expected Kat and Devin would be among them but they weren't.

As I watched, one of the policemen who had gone into the store came out and scanned the parking lot. When he spotted the motorhome, he nodded and headed in my direction. As he walked across the lot, I was hoping he was going to one of the other motorhomes parked nearby.

But he wasn't. He walked up to my door, knocked and said, "Police. Open up, I need to talk to you."

I opened the door.

"How can I help you, officer?"

He pulled a notepad from his back pocket.

"Your name is?"

"Walker. John Walker."

"Mr. Walker, do you have any ID? A driver's license?"

"I do."

I reached into my wallet, pulled out my license and handed it to him. He looked at it, wrote something in his notepad and handed it back to me.

"Mr. Walker, why did you come to Walmart today?"

It was a strange question but an easy one to answer.

"To get groceries."

"And did you come here alone?"

"No, I came with two women. Has anything happened to them?"

The officer smiled. "We'll get to that later. Can you tell me the names of the two women?"

"Sure, the taller one is Kat. The shorter one is Devin."

He looked down at his notepad. "Would that be Katrina Chesnokov and Devin McSweeney?"

I nodded. I knew Kat's last name was Chesnokov. I didn't know what Devin's was but figured if the officer said it was McSweeney that was probably it.

He smiled and closed his notepad. "Thank you. That's all I need."

He started to turn and walk away, but I said, "Wait! What's going on inside? Have Kat and Devin been arrested for something?"

He turned back to face me. "Mr. Walker, the two women haven't been arrested, nor have they been injured. They were involved in an incident and, for their safety, we're verifying their story before we release them. If everything checks out, they'll be free to go."

An incident in the store? That didn't sound good.

"Can I go in and talk to them?"

"No, we aren't allowing anyone inside the store right now. Just sit tight. They'll be out in few minutes."

He turned and started to walk away but stopped and came back. He looked around to make sure no one but me could hear what he was about to say. "Mr. Walker, do you have life insurance?"

I didn't and wondered if he was going to try to sell me some. "No, why?"

He looked behind him again making sure no one was close enough to hear our conversation.

"Those two ladies you're with, their fathers are known to be, let's say, very protective of their daughters. People who cross them often have a need for life insurance. If you plan to stay around them long, you might want to get some, if you get my drift."

He handed me his card. "If things get out of hand, give me a call. Otherwise, be careful."

He nodded and walked away.

I already knew about Kat's father. He definitely was someone you didn't want to cross. Devin's father was another story. I'd only just met her and didn't even know her last name until the officer mentioned it. McSweeney sounded Irish. It would fit with Devin's story of being in an Irish Travelers clan.

She hadn't mentioned her father or made any reference to the dangers he might pose. I doubted she would talk about it if I asked her, so my plan was to follow the officer's advice. Be careful.

Around both of them.

As I watched the officer walk back to the store, I saw the paramedics come out pushing a gurney. A man with a large bandage covering the top of his head was strapped to it. The paramedics slid the gurney into the back of the EMT van and drove away, siren blasting and lights flashing.

A policeman stepped out of the store and walked up to the officer who had just spoken to me. He pointed at the motorhome and asked a question. The officer flipped open his notebook and shared his notes. After about a minute, the two parted ways. The one I'd spoken to went back inside the store. The other one went to his car, started it up and headed in my direction.

I expected him to stop and ask me more questions. He slowed down as he drove past the motorhome but kept going. I watched until he pulled out of the Walmart lot and headed east.

I turned back toward Walmart's front door and saw Kat and Devin heading my way. They were pushing a shopping cart filled with groceries. Relieved that they were apparently uninjured and free to go, I stepped out of the motorhome and trotted across the lot to meet them.

As soon as I got close, Devin said, "You're not going to believe what happened in there."

Chapter Sixteen

Devin was doing all the talking. "So we were shopping, just minding our own business. We'd gotten the chicken and the wine like we planned, and then got bacon and eggs for breakfast. Kat didn't think you had a skillet to cook the bacon, so we went over to where they have kitchen stuff.

"There weren't many people in that part of the store. Just us and a young girl. She was about twelve, by herself. She was doing what most twelve-year-olds do in a store, touching everything.

"Anyway, so we're looking at frying pans and this guy comes up and grabs the girl by the hair and starts dragging her away. She's screaming, 'Help me, help me!' but there's no one around to help her, except for us.

"Kat had just put an eight inch cast iron skillet in our shopping cart and when she saw the guy dragging the girl away, she picked it up and went over and tapped the guy on the side of the head with it.

"His knees buckled and he almost let the girl go but he didn't. He turned and cussed Kat. Told her to stay away or else he was going to hurt her. Then he started dragging the girl again."

Devin took a deep breath then continued with her story.

"I don't know if you know this but Kat doesn't like being told what to do, especially by a big gomer dragging a little girl by the hair. So she walked up to him and tapped him on the head again. With the iron skillet. This time a bit harder.

"He hit the floor twitching like he'd been struck by lightning. His eyes were open but he wasn't seeing anything. He let go of the girl as soon as he was hit and she got up and ran off to her mother who had come looking for her.

"By then a crowd had gathered, including the store manager and an off duty fire fighter. Someone called 9-1-1, and the police showed up.

"At first they thought Kat had assaulted the man, what with her standing over him holding the skillet. The police grabbed her but witnesses came forward and told the them what really happened—that it was Kat who saved the little girl from the man.

"He was still unconscious on the floor and didn't have much to say. But the police found his driver's license and called it in. They learned he had been released from prison three days earlier and was a registered sex offender.

"The assistant manager said they had a video that would show everything that happened, and he agreed to show it to the police. After watching it and talking to me and Kat separately and listening to witnesses, the cops had us sign statements and said we were free to go.

"The officer in charge said that, because they had the video and because the guy was a repeat offender out on parole, there probably wouldn't be a trial. It'd be a plea deal and we wouldn't need to testify. But if there was a trial, we would be called.

"The store manager saw our shopping full of groceries and he said he'd be honored to personally check us out at the register. He rang it all up and said we didn't have to pay because Kat had saved that little girl."

Devin finished off her story by saying, "The end."

By then we'd made it back to the motorhome. Kat went in first, followed by Devin. I grabbed the groceries and started carrying them in. Devin put them away while Kat sat on the couch.

She hadn't spoken a word while Devin was telling me the story. But now that we were back inside the motorhome, she opened up. "All I wanted was to buy some food. Just go in there, pick up a few things and come back out. But no, that pervert had to grab the little girl. He did it right in front of me. He was thinking I wasn't going to do anything. Just stand there and let it happen.

"He was wrong. In my world, you don't do things like that and get away with it."

She took a deep breath and stared out the window. Devin and I finished putting away the food. When we were done, Kat looked up at us and said, "Time to hit the road. And, Walker, I'm driving."

I wasn't sure whether it would be safe for her to drive in her current state of mind, but then again it might not be safe for me to try to stop her. Driving might help her get over what had happened in the store and that would be a good thing.

"Sure, you drive. Campground's close, right?"

She didn't answer me. Instead she turned to Devin. "Call Ho Hum; see if they can fit us in tonight."

Without waiting for a reply, she moved to the driver's seat, adjusted the mirrors and started the motor. She put the motorhome in gear and said, "Buckle up, bitches."

Chapter Seventeen

It was probably good Kat was driving. She knew where we were going and I didn't.

A mile past Walmart, she took a left and stayed on US 98 as it headed west into a part of Florida known as the Forgotten Coast. The road narrowed to a two lane blacktop with open pastures on our right and a thick pine forest on our left.

Five miles in, the pastures on our right gave way to more pine forests. The tall trees and thick woods on both sides of the road created the illusion of traveling in a narrow pine tree tunnel at sixty miles an hour.

Kat hadn't spoken since we'd left the Walmart lot but I could see the tension drain out of her body as she relaxed her grip on the steering wheel. For the first time since we got on this stretch of road, she turned to me and smiled. She said nothing, and then returned her focus to driving.

I took this as my cue to say something. "You want me to drive?"

She shook her head. "No, not yet. But I do want you to change seats with Devin. I need to talk with her."

Devin was sitting behind Kat on the couch and wouldn't be able to carry on a conversation over the noise of the tires on the road.

"Are you sure you don't want me to drive? I could take the wheel and you could sit back there with her. "

She looked in my direction, no smile this time. "Walker, change seats with Devin. Do it now, please."

Not wanting to upset her, especially while she was driving, I got up and moved to the couch. Devin looked at me and asked, "What's up?"

I pointed to the now vacant passenger seat. "Kat wants you up there."

Devin didn't ask why. She grabbed her phone and headed up front. Almost as soon as she sat down, Kat asked her, "Were they able to fit us in?"

"Yeah, they're holding a place for us. Said we need to get there before sundown or the gate will be closed."

Kat stepped on the gas. "We'll make it."

Thirty minutes later, I felt the motorhome slow and heard the ticking of the turn signal. Kat was braking and pulling over into a dirt driveway. She brought the motorhome to a full stop, unbuckled her seat belt and turned to me. "You can drive now."

I didn't question why she suddenly wanted me to drive, I was just happy she was letting me take over. We traded places. She moved to the couch and I moved to the driver's seat. When I was sure she was settled in, I put the motorhome in gear, checked for oncoming traffic, and pulled back out on the road. As soon as I got the motorhome up to speed, I set the cruise control.

I looked over at Devin and whispered, "Where are we going?"

She pointed ahead. "Ho Hum RV park. Sixty miles that way. Just stay on this road and you'll see it on your left. It'll be an easy drive, just watch out for deer."

With that said she got up and moved back to the couch

and sat down beside Kat. I could hear them whispering but couldn't make out what they were saying. I turned my attention back to the road. Up ahead a sign read, 'Welcome to Tate's Hell.'

Had either Devin or Kat been in the seat beside me, I would have asked them about the sign. I was sure one of them would know why this part of Florida was called Hell. But I didn't want to bother them so I didn't ask.

We'd gone thirty miles since leaving Perry and the Walmart lot. We'd had only seen five other cars on this road. All were heading in the opposite direction. They were leaving Hell just as we were entering it.

Chapter Eighteen

The sun had begun to set and the towering pines on our left and right created long shadows that crisscrossed the road ahead. The patterns of dark and light were making it difficult for me to see objects in the distance.

Devin had told me to watch for deer. I'd already seen a few hiding in the trees. As darkness fell, they would get brave and venture out onto the road creating a hazard that would be hard to avoid at sixty miles an hour. I didn't want to hit a deer. It wouldn't be good for the deer or the motorhome. But with the sun setting in the west, directly in front me, it was becoming more and more difficult to watch the road and look for deer at the same time. I needed a copilot. I leaned back and called out, "I need help up here."

I could hear the girls talking, probably trying to decide which one was going to come up front to help me. It didn't take long for them to make a decision. Kat took the passenger seat.

"What do you need?"

I pointed down the road. "It's starting to get dark and I'm worried about deer. The sun's in my eyes and I'm afraid I'll hit one."

Kat nodded. "You need to slow down. There's no one behind us so don't worry about holding up traffic."

I lifted my foot off the gas and let the motorhome burn off some speed. When I got it down to fifty, I reset the cruise control.

With Kat beside me, I decided to ask her about something that had been bothering me. "Why aren't there any other cars on this road? I've driven thirty miles and only seen one."

She didn't answer right away. I wasn't even sure she'd heard my question. But eventually she answered. "This road doesn't connect to any major cities or tourist attractions. No tourists means not much traffic.

"The few people who live around here know better than to drive this road after dark. It's eighty miles of wilderness with almost no place to stop and no way to get help if something happens. Smart people don't drive it at night."

I nodded. "And yet here we are, driving the road that smart people avoid. Tell me why."

This time she answered quicker. "We're driving this road because I wanted to get as far away from Walmart as we could before we set up camp. I didn't want to take the chance that anyone who saw what happened back there would come looking for us.

"I wanted to spend the night somewhere quiet. With no crowds, no kids, no trouble makers. That's where we're going. When we get there, you'll see what I mean. You'll be glad we went a little farther than planned and took this road."

Turns out she was right.

Fifteen miles further on, Kat had me slow and take a left into the driveway of the Ho Hum RV Park. At first glance, it didn't look like much, but maybe Kat knew something I didn't. But really, it didn't matter to me what the park was like. I was happy to be finally getting off the road.

It'd been a long day with a lot of unexpected surprises,

what with the disguised pregnant teenage girl, the extended trip to Niceville that would add almost a thousand miles to our trip, and the skillet episode in Walmart.

So, yeah, it'd been a long day and I was happy to pull into the Ho Hum RV Park. I started to get out, intending to sign in at the office, but Kat stopped me. "Let Devin go in and take care of it. She knows the owners."

Devin was already up off the couch and heading out the door. I didn't bother to try to stop her. As far as I was concerned, this was the Kat and Devin show and I was just playing a bit part.

While waiting for Devin's return, Bob, my four-legged travel companion, came up front to join us. He'd been sleeping in the back ever since we left Walmart. Now that we were stopped, he wanted to see where we'd be spending the night.

Normally, he'd jump up on the passenger seat then place his paws on the dash so he could look out. But with Kat in the passenger seat, his path was blocked. He looked at me, meowed softly, then turned and jumped into Kat's lap. She started petting him and, for Bob, this was way better than looking out the window.

Ten minutes later, Devin walked out of the Ho Hum office with a smile on her face and a small folder in her left hand. She walked to my window and tapped on the glass. I rolled it down and she said, "They gave us a choice spot. Right on the water. It's not far so I'll walk over there and you can follow. When we get there, pull straight in."

She took off walking, not waiting to see if I had any questions. When she was a good thirty feet in front of us, I started the motorhome and moved in her direction.

We passed two rows of campsites before we reached ours.

Our site was the first one to the left of the fishing pier. Devin walked to the back of it where it met the beach and guided me in. Since we didn't have to back in, I didn't need guiding, but I let her do it anyway.

With our motorhome facing the water, our windshield had a direct view of the Gulf of Mexico. We'd be able to sit inside and look out over it and hear the tides come and go throughout the night.

Devin came back using the side door. "So what do you think? Do you like the site?"

The question was easy to answer. "Yeah, this is a nice site. Was it expensive?"

She shook her head. "No, not at all. Less than forty dollars a night."

I pulled out my wallet thinking I needed to pay her, but she said, "No, keep your money. I got this one. You can get the next."

I was hoping the next one would be at Devin's home, where we'd be picking up the package for Kat's father. But I wasn't banking on it. I expected a few more surprises before we got there.

With the motorhome parked in the site, I went about the process of setting up camp. The first step was to make sure Bob was secure. He was still in Kat's lap and didn't look like he would be going anywhere soon. That was good because when I pushed the button for the slide room, it would move the driver's side wall outward, opening up space inside the motorhome. As long as Bob wasn't in the way when the wall moved out, he'd be safe.

After I got the slide deployed, I grabbed the keys from the ignition and headed outside to hook up shore power. Our site had full hookups—water, electric, sewer and cable

TV. I hooked up the water and electric, which was really all we needed. But I figured since the campground had cable TV, I might as well hook it up. With cable, we'd be able to check local weather and news without having to crank up the TV antenna on the roof.

Before going back inside, I did a quick walk around to make sure the tires looked good and we weren't leaking any fluids. I do this almost every time we stop. With my house on wheels, I want to catch problems early before they leave me stranded on the road.

Other than a few thousand dead insects on the front cap, everything looked good. Standing in front of the motorhome, I realized how special this park was. Our campsite was a foot from the sands of the Gulf of Mexico. Unlike the busier parts of Florida, there were no high rises in the distance, no flashing lights, no gaudy tourist attractions, and no low flying planes or traffic noise. Just peace and quiet.

Kat had said I'd be happy when we got there. Now I knew what she had meant.

Back inside, she'd opened a bottle of wine and poured three glasses. She was holding one, and Devin had one as well. Kat nodded for me to pick up mine.

When I did, she raised her glass and said, "Here's to Walker and his motorhome. Our knight in shining armor."

Devin tapped her glass against Kat's and I did the same. For the next few minutes, we relaxed as we watched the light show outside created by the setting sun as its rays bounced off slow moving waves and the distant clouds on the horizon.

Kat finished her glass and poured another. She reached over to fill mine but I stopped her. "No more for me right now. I need to go for a walk. You want to go?"

She shook her head. "No, I'm just going to sit here and chill. What about you, Devin? You want to go for a stroll with Walker?"

Devin looked at me and winked. "I'll go for a walk with him. But only if he promises to hold my hand."

Kat laughed. "Walker, you don't mind holding her hand, do you?"

"No, not at all. In fact, I'll be glad to hold her hand all the way out to the end of the fishing pier. But after that, no promises."

I looked at Devin. "You can swim, can't you?"

"Yeah I can swim. But I might not need to. Could be you're the one who ends up in the water."

I smiled. "Yeah, right."

I reached for the door. "I'll be back in a few minutes."

From behind me I heard Devin say, "Wait for me."

I opened the door and looked back. Kat was sitting on the couch, wine glass in hand. She smiled and mouthed the words, "Be careful."

That's exactly what I planned to be. Careful. With both Kat and Devin.

Chapter Nineteen

When I camp, I like to get out and walk through the campground so I can check out all the other RVs. It's a good way to see who your neighbors are for the night and to get the lay of the land. Since I was camping with two women, I wouldn't be using the bathroom in the motorhome. Not enough privacy for that. That's one of the reasons I wanted to take a walk, to find the campground bathhouse.

I didn't mention this to Devin who was walking with me. In fact, I didn't say anything, I just walked. She walked behind me at first, but soon caught up and walked by my side. We had reached the end of the first row of RVs when she said, "You should have seen her. She picked up the skillet and popped that guy on the head. I was afraid she was going to kill him."

I knew who she was talking about but I asked her anyway. "You're talking about Kat, right?"

"Yeah, back in the store. When she hit that guy I thought she was going to kill him. When she hit him the second time, I was sure he was dead.

"I was glad when he didn't try to get up because she would have finished him off."

I nodded. "She saved the little girl?"

"Yeah, she did. But she almost killed the guy doing it."

I nodded but didn't say anything.

"She has anger issues. You know about that, don't you?

You know not to get her mad, right?"

Again I nodded. "People keep telling me that. They say, 'Don't get her mad.' But I don't know why. I've never seen her get really angry."

"You would have if you had been in the store with us today. She went from normal to total psycho killer in a flash. Normal one minute then cracking the guy upside the head with a skillet the next.

"I'm telling you, you don't want to make her mad."

I didn't know what to say, so I kept my mouth shut.

Devin kept talking. "So are you and Kat living together?"

"No, why would you think that?"

"Well, you said you live in your motorhome full time and Kat's traveling with you. I figured you and her have something going on. Am I right?"

I wasn't sure why she was asking these kinds of questions, but I knew how to answer them.

"You're wrong. Kat and I are just friends. Nothing more. Her father asked me to help her find a motorhome, and that's what I've been doing."

She smiled. "So you're not dating. Are you saying she wouldn't be jealous if you started seeing someone else? She wouldn't get mad?"

I didn't know the answer to that question, so I changed the subject. "What's in the package we're supposed to pick up for Kat's father?"

Devin shook her head. "I can't tell you."

"Why not?"

"Because he wouldn't want me to. That's reason enough for me. You know how he is."

I did know. He had sworn me to secrecy when I worked for him. He'd personally warned me my life would be at risk if I told anyone what I was doing for him.

That secrecy had created a rift between me and Kat. She wanted to know what her father had me doing and I wouldn't tell. She'd even threatened me with a gun and I still refused. I'd almost made her mad but not enough for her to shoot me or whack me upside the head with a skillet.

"Devin, I understand you can't tell me what's in the package. Can you at least tell me how big it is? Will it fit in one of the overhead compartments in the motorhome?"

She shook her head. "Not telling. You'll just have to wait and see."

We had walked the three rows of campsites and were nearing the campground office where the bathhouse was located. She pointed at the women's side. "I'm going in. Wait for me out here."

As soon as the door closed behind her, I went in the men's side and used the facilities. I washed up and was back outside before Devin returned.

I was standing right where she had left me when she came out. She said, "Pretty nice place. Even the bathrooms are clean. How was yours?"

"Clean."

"Good, now hold my hand like you promised."

She grabbed my hand and took off walking in the direction of our campsite. I had no choice but to go with her, close by her side. She had short arms. As we got near the motorhome, she asked, "We going to walk to the end of the pier?"

It sounded like a good idea to me.

"Yeah, let's do that."

Still holding my hand, she stepped up onto the pier decking and we walked the full two hundred and fifty feet to the viewing platform at the end.

She let go of my hand and sat down on the bench that wrapped around the rails of the pier. She tapped the space beside her. "Sit. We need to have a talk."

I didn't mind sitting, but wasn't sure I wanted to have a 'talk', so I said, "Are you sure we need to talk?"

"Yeah, I think we do. There's something you need to know. It's kind of important."

I sighed, shook my head and sat down on the bench beside her. "Okay, talk."

She took my hand again, looked into my eyes and said, "This is all a big con. And you're the target."

Chapter Twenty

"What exactly am I being conned out of? Tell me that."

Devin frowned. "I haven't figured that part out yet. But I know Kat. She's running some kind of con on you. That's how she works."

I didn't know if she was right or not but I wanted to see what else she had to say. "Well, let's suppose you're right, that she is running some kind of con on me. What could she possibly gain from me?"

Devin nervously looked back at my motorhome. From her spot on the couch, Kat would be able see us sitting side by side out on the pier. She wouldn't be able to hear what we were saying, but she could see us talking.

Devin looked out over the water and whispered, "Normally, a con involves money. So how much do you have and where is it?"

I wasn't surprised by her question. If she were the one running the con, she'd want to know about the money. Who had it and where it was held. Rather than tell her the truth, I said, "I don't have any money. A few hundred dollars in my wallet and a maybe a thousand in my checking account, that's pretty much it."

I could see the disappointment in her eyes. "That's all you have? How can you afford to live in your motorhome with no money?"

It was a question people asked me often. I told Devin the

same thing I tell everyone else.

"It's not hard. My only expense is food and gas. I put the gas on a credit card and take on odd jobs to make enough to buy food and pay the monthly credit card bill."

"So you're basically broke?"

I nodded. "Yeah, broke, unemployed, and living in a motorhome with my cat. That's me."

She looked at me for a moment then said, "You don't really have anything worth taking, do you?"

"No. I don't. Just my motorhome and Bob."

That's all she needed to hear. No need for her to waste any more time on me. She stood. "We probably need to get back."

Instead of waiting for me, she headed back to the motorhome, this time showing no interest in holding my hand. Now that she thought I was broke, it appeared she'd lost interest in me. I was fine with that.

Back at the motorhome, Devin went in first and I followed. Kat was still on the couch. Same place she'd been when Devin and I left for our walk. Bob had joined her and was sitting in her lap. The bottle of wine that had been half full when we left was now empty.

"So, did you enjoy your walk?"

Devin nodded. "Yeah, I did. Walker was a real gentleman. Didn't even try to push me off the pier."

"That's nice. But I think I need to go for a walk now."

She looked up at me. "What's it going to take to get this cat off my lap?"

I reached over and touched Bob's head. "Come on, Bob, let's go check your food."

When he heard the word 'food', his ears perked up. I'd gotten his attention. But he remained in Kat's lap. I then tried the secret word that I knew would get him to move. "Bob, you want a treat?"

That's all it took. When he heard the word 'treat', he meowed loudly and jumped down onto the floor. He watched me expectantly, hoping to see me open the kitchen cabinet where I kept his bag of kitty treats.

I didn't disappoint. I opened the cabinet, grabbed the little yellow bag of treats and pulled out three small, fished shaped morsels. Bob came to attention. His eyes tightly focused on the treats in my hand.

I held one up so he could see it and then threw it down the hall toward the back of the coach. He launched into the air, chasing the treat as it slid along the floor. It took him just three steps to catch up with it, hit it with his paw and pop it into his mouth.

He bit it in half and swallowed. Then he ran back to me and sat at my feet. He looked up and let out a short meow telling me he was ready for the next one.

He knew that, when it came to getting treats, he always got three. No more, no less. Always three. With one down, there'd be two more to go.

As with the first one, I held the treat between my fingers so he could see it. I moved my hand slowly side-to-side as Bob watched, moving his head in sync with my hand. It was a game we played—me holding a treat while he tried to guess which way I'd throw it.

This time, I tossed it toward the front of the coach, sliding it on the floor toward the driver's seat. As before, Bob chased it down, hit it with his paw and popped it into his mouth.

As soon as he swallowed it, he trotted back to me, licking his lips along the way. He took his position in front of me, wondering where the next one would go.

Before I threw it, I turned to the girls and said, "Watch this."

Instead of sliding the treat on the floor like I had with the first two, I threw the third one high up in air, above Bob's head. His eyes followed it as it went up, patiently watching and calculating where it might land. When the treat started its downward trajectory, he leapt three feet into the air and caught it in his mouth.

It was an impressive move for a twenty pound cat in the narrow confines of a motorhome hallway. I congratulated him. "Good job, Bob. You could be a circus kitty."

He sat on the floor, licking his paws, quite pleased with himself and three kitty treats he had just consumed.

The girls were impressed. Kat spoke first. "That was amazing! Did you teach him that?"

"No, he learned it on his own. The first time he did it, I think it surprised him as much as it did me. After that, it just became part of the treat ritual. He now wants the third one to be airborne. I do my best not to disappoint him."

Devin, who had yet to sit down since coming back inside, asked, "Can I try it? Can I throw him one?"

I shook my head. "No, not now. If I give him more than three at a time, he'll expect to get more than three next time. I don't want to go down that road so no more tonight. But you can do it tomorrow."

Kat stood and stretched. "I need to go for a walk. Walker, will you go with me?"

After my little walk and talk with Devin, it would be

interesting to hear what Kat had to say. "Yeah, I'll go with you."

The sun had set and it had gotten dark outside. I grabbed a flashlight and headed for the door. I waited there while Kat pulled on her shoes.

Two minutes later, we were outside, heading toward the bathhouses at the front of the park.

Kat's first question was, "What'd she tell you?"

Chapter Twenty-one

"She said you were running on a con on me."

Kat laughed. "Yeah, that sounds like something she'd say. What else?"

"She said most cons involve money and she wanted to know if I had any."

"Again, that sounds like her. What did you tell her?"

"I told her I was broke and unemployed, just barely getting by."

Kat snorted. "Did she believe you?"

"I think so. She didn't ask any more questions after that. She seemed disappointed."

"Good, good. I like the way this is going. This is going to be fun."

I wasn't sure what she meant by 'fun' but I wanted to find out. "Fun? In what way?"

I looked up and noticed we had walked all the way to the bathhouse. It seemed further away when I walked with Devin but Kat and I had reached it in no time. She pointed at the ground and said, "Wait for me here. When I get back, I'll tell you all about it."

She went inside and I waited.

A few minutes later, she came back out and said, "You ready to go back?"

"No, not until you tell me what's going on with you and Devin. You said something about this was going to be fun?"

She smiled. "Oh yeah, that. It's a long story, but basically whenever Devin and I got together, one of us would be running some kind of con and the other would try to figure it out. It was like a game between us.

"We never tried to hurt anyone with the cons. They were just a way to sharpen our skills and see what we could get away with.

"She took it more seriously than I did and she always thought I was up to something. It would drive her crazy trying to figure out what I was running, even when I wasn't running one. She didn't believe me when I told her I was giving up the business and going straight.

"It's been almost eight years and she still thinks I'm running cons on people. That's why she thinks I'm running one on you.

"But maybe she's right. I did kind of con you into taking this trip. I misled you about why we were going and how long we'd be on the road. I knew we were going to pick up Devin in Crystal River and I knew we'd have to drive to her place to pick up the package for my father. I knew that, instead of one or two days on the road, we'll probably be gone for a week.

"I could have told you all that before we left but what fun would that have been? This way it's an adventure. One you'll remember for a long time.

"So yeah, maybe I'm running a little con on you but not to hurt you. But we don't want Devin to know that. We want her to think that I'm running a bigger con. It'll drive her crazy trying to figure it out. So just play along. Okay?"

It didn't bother me too much that Kat had misled me

about the nature of our trip. Going to different and interesting places in the motorhome, especially accompanied by two single women, wasn't something I was going to complain about.

I'd known Kat long enough to know she was probably telling the truth when she said she wasn't running a longer con on me. She knew I wasn't broke, but neither was she. She had plenty of money and if she needed more her father would give it to her. He'd made that clear before he let her leave Key West with me.

So maybe, instead of running a con, all she really wanted was a road trip with a little adventure. That was fine with me.

I hadn't answered Kat, so she asked again. "Walker, you won't tell her, will you?"

"No Kat, I won't. I'll play along."

"Good. Now let's go back to the motorhome. I'm hungry."

Devin was sitting on the couch when we got back. The bag of Bob's treats was in her lap and she had her hand inside the bag. Bob was on the floor near her feet, crunching on what I presumed was a kitty treat.

"You caught me," she said.

I nodded. "You found the treats and gave him one."

"It's not my fault. He started crying when you left and I didn't know what to do. I asked what he wanted and when I mentioned 'treat', he said what sounded like 'yes'. So I got the bag out and gave him one. Then he wanted another and I couldn't stop myself. He loves those things and kept wanting more. But I only gave him three. You can check the bag if you don't believe me."

She held the bag out. I took it from her and said, "Maybe it'd be best if I hid these, just in case Bob tries to convince you he needs more."

I took the bag back to my bedroom. I wasn't really planning on hiding the treats there; I just wanted to make sure nothing in the room had been disturbed while I was out walking with Kat. Hiding the treats gave me an excuse to do so without raising any suspicion.

I checked the closet and the bed. Everything looked just as I had left it. I put the treats in the top drawer of the bedside table and went back up front. The girls had gotten the chicken out of the fridge along with the Caesar salad kit. Kat was opening another bottle of wine while Devin was carving the chicken.

Kat turned to me. "Sit down, we're about to eat." Not wanting to argue, I took a seat at the dining table.

Devin set the plates and silverware, and Kat poured each of us another glass of wine. Then we proceeded to eat.

The chicken was cold but tasty. The Caesar salad added a nice touch. The conversation was interesting, mostly between Devin and Kat talking about their younger years together.

When we finished the chicken, Devin cut us each a large slice of the Key lime pie she'd picked up at Walmart. Even though it was from the frozen food section, it was pretty good.

Kat stayed busy keeping our wine glasses full. I begged off after my second glass, saying I was a lightweight and didn't want to wake up with a hangover. That didn't bother her one bit. "Good, it'll mean more wine for me and Devin."

When the girls started on their third bottle, I figured they were juiced up enough to tell me about the Trailer

Monkeys. They had mentioned them earlier but never got around to telling the full story. I decided to see if they would now. "Devin, tell me about the Trailer Monkeys."

She laughed, pointed at Kat and said, "Squally and Pico. You want me to tell the story?"

Kat nodded. "Yeah, go ahead."

Devin took a sip of wine and started in. "Squally and Pico. They're brothers. Squally was the good looking one, Pico was the brains. They were always trying to figure out ways to make a quick buck.

"We met them when we bought a trailer that was too big for our truck to haul. We'd been looking for someone to tow it and a guy at the local Shell station gave us a number and said to ask for Pico.

"We called and they said they could do it. They showed up on time, gave us a decent price, and moved the trailer for us. Long story short, we started using them to move other trailers. Word soon got around that Pico and Squally were in the trailer moving business and snowbirds and park owners started calling with towing jobs.

"Pico decided they needed to come up with a business name and get it painted with a phone number on the side of their truck. That way, people would know who to call.

"Squally, the one without the brains, was the one who came up with the name. He saw a TV show where a bunch of mechanics were called 'grease monkeys', and he liked the way it sounded. So he figured 'Trailer Monkeys' was what they should be called.

Pico wasn't sure about the name, but Squally went ahead and had it painted on the truck. He had a friend who was an artist and he agreed to paint the name along with two grinning monkeys in exchange for a case of Pabst Blue

Ribbon beer.

"Squally didn't tell Pico he was getting artwork put on the truck. He figured that once the paint was dry, it'd be too late for Pico to do anything about it. As it turned out, Pico liked what he saw and they became known as the Trailer Monkeys.

"Not too long after, Kat here started dating Squally. He was definitely good looking, but, as Kat will tell you, he wasn't real smart. Fortunately, you didn't need a lot of brains when all you did was move trailers around.

"They dated for about three months. For a while there, it looked like things were getting pretty serious. But then Ashley showed up."

Kat interrupted Devin's story with a long 'boo' upon hearing Ashley's name. Then she took a drink of wine and let Devin continue with her tale.

"Ashley was a city girl and Squally thought she was something else. Blonde hair, blue eyes, always wearing tight jeans. With her city girl make-up and sweet perfume, it was hard for Squally to stay away.

"He told Kat he was conflicted. He liked Kat a lot, but he yearned to be with Ashley. The reality was he was already doing a bit more than just yearning for Ashley. He was dating her behind Kat's back.

"When Kat found out, she cut him loose. But not before she threatened to do some real cutting on him with her pearl handled knife. She pulled it out and showed Squally the blade, and he wisely beat a path to the door.

"So with Kat out of the picture, Squally started hanging around Ashley, buying her flowers, writing her poetry, even going to the mall with her to shop for shoes. He loved being with her but was finding it was expensive to court her. She was a high maintenance girl and she expected Squally to spend money on her. Money he didn't have.

"She out and out told him, 'If you want to be with me, you'll need to make more money.' Problem was Squally didn't know how to make more money, and he was afraid he was going to lose Ashley. He thought about getting a second job, but there weren't too many places wanting to hire someone with his minimal skill set.

"Then, one day, when he was watching TV, he saw a story about a guy who got a million dollar payout because he got bit by a snake while shopping in a department store.

"Squally figured that for a million dollars he wouldn't mind getting bit by a snake. He mentioned it to a drinking buddy and between them they came up with a plan. His buddy would go out in the swamp and get a snake. Not just any snake though. He'd get one small enough to fit in the front pocket of Squally's cargo shorts. To get maximum money from the store, they figured the snake needed to be poisonous, but not enough to kill Squally.

"His friend said, 'No problem. I know all about snakes. I'll get you a good one.'

"He showed up two days later carrying an ice chest that had three snakes and a cold six pack of beer in it. He told Squally the beer was there to keep the snakes cool. Said they'd be less apt to bite that way. Squally could have his pick of the snakes for fifty dollars.

"Squally didn't much like snakes and he didn't know much about them. He sure didn't want to spend fifty dollars on one. But he figured spending fifty would be a good investment if he got millions back in return. He gave his friend two twenties and a ten, and picked out the smallest snake. Gray with black spots on its back.

"Not one to waste time, Squally put the snake in a purple Crown Royal bag and pulled the gold drawstrings tight. He put the bag in his pants pocket and headed to the big home improvement store in Tallahassee. He was in a hurry because he was worried the snake wasn't in good health. It felt cold and wasn't moving around much.

"But that soon changed. Being in his pocket, up against his body, the snake warmed up. By the time Squally got to the store in Tallahassee, the snake was feeling pretty lively, moving around trying to get out of the bag in his pocket.

"Squally hurried into the store, headed over to the plant section, and when he was sure no one was looking, he reached into his pocket and loosened the draw strings on the bag. His plan was to grab the snake, let it bite him on the hand, then call out for help.

"Unfortunately, the snake had different plans. As soon as Squally opened the Crown Royal bag, the snake crawled out and headed for a small hole in his pocket.

"Squally wasn't wearing underwear that day and when he felt the snake head for his man parts, he slipped his hand between his cargo shorts and belly to try to grab the snake. The snake, feeling threatened by the big hand coming at him, struck. But it wasn't Squally's hand that got bit.

"His screams attracted a crowd—including several people who saw a small snake crawl out of his shorts. One of them, a farmer from nearby Woodville, quickly dispatched it with the heel of his boot.

"When the store manager walked up, Squally was on the floor, pants down around his knees, screaming about a snake bite. The manager quickly covered his exposed parts with a shopping bag and called 9-1-1.

"Squally was taken to a nearby hospital. The paramedics

who picked him up had wisely grabbed the remains of the snake. At the hospital, it was identified as a pygmy rattler. Small but quite venomous.

"They shot Squally up with anti-venom and pain killers and moved him into a private room. The doctor working his case warned him that a snake bite on his private parts might cause him to lose the ability to have sex.

"Squally was distraught and would have been suicidal if it weren't for the thought that he'd be getting a million dollars from the store as a result of the snake bite on his weenie.

"With the heavy dose of painkillers inside him, Squally went to sleep knowing that soon the store manager would show up with his million dollar check.

"But his first visitor wasn't the store manager. It was a detective from the Tallahassee police department. The store had provided him an interesting video recorded the day Squally had ventured into the garden department. The video clearly showed Squally had brought his own snake into the store and it was his fault he had been bit.

"The store wasn't going to give Squally any money. In fact, they were thinking about suing him for the problems he caused that day.

"What made it even worse was the store had given copies of the video to the local news stations. They wasted no time in airing it, playing it over and over, often in slow motion so viewers could watch Squally's expressions go from joy to sheer terror as the snake made its way to his nether regions.

"When Ashley found out what Squally had done, she was furious. His newfound TV notoriety reflected poorly on her choice of men. She decided it was best not to visit him in the hospital and to end their relationship immediately.

"Pico wasn't too happy either. Not only did he have to

come up with the money to cover Squally's medical bills, the news media had learned of the boy's business name and they were mentioning it every time they showed the video. The 'Snake Bit Trailer Monkey' story lived on for weeks.

"Eventually the local news found other stories to follow and interest in Squally's video died down. At least it seemed that way at first. But then the prank calls started coming in. People would call the Trailer Monkeys' phone number and ask things like whether Squally wanted to buy another snake and tell him there were easier ways to get his man parts to swell up.

"This was particularly hard on Squally, who not only lost his beloved Ashley, but lost use of his manhood for almost six months. The funny thing was people remembered the Trailer Monkeys' name, even months later. And when they needed a trailer moved, they'd call the Monkeys. Their business actually improved after the snake bite. But Squally was never the same. No longer outgoing, he's was reserved around strangers and afraid of places where there was a possibility of snakes."

Devin smiled and said, "And that my friend, is the tale of the Snake Bit Trailer Monkeys."

Kat, who had finished two more glasses of wine during the telling, burst out laughing. She had snorted and giggled through most of the story but held back her big laugh until the end. I could see the humor in the story, but, as a man, it was hard for me to laugh about another man getting bit in his nether regions by a snake. Still, the peals of laughter from Devin and Kat were contagious. I eventually joined in.

Our laughter was interrupted by the first few bars of Darth Vader's theme song coming from Kat's phone. She looked at the display and said, "Be quiet, I've got to take this."

She held the phone to her ear and said, "Hi Daddy, is anything wrong?"

Chapter Twenty-two

"No, I'm fine. I'm here with Walker, in Carrabelle. In his motorhome.

"No, he wasn't in the store with us. It was just me and Devin.

"I know, but I couldn't just stand there and let the guy take the little girl. I had to stop him.

"Yes, he was still alive when we left.

"Okay, you can talk to him."

She held the phone out to me. "It's my father; he wants to talk to you."

I didn't want to talk to her father. His calling and asking to speak to me was not a good sign. But there was no way I would disrespect him by not taking to him when he specifically asked for me. Reluctantly, I took the phone.

I didn't want to address him using his first name. I knew it was Boris and at our last meeting he said to call him that. But it seemed too informal. So I just said, "Hello?"

He didn't bother asking me how I was. He just said, "Walker, you're supposed to keep my daughter out of trouble. That's why I wanted you to get her out of Key West. To keep her out of trouble. But apparently you're not able to do that.

"I just got a call from an associate who told me she assaulted a man in a Walmart store today. The man she attacked might even die. Tell me how you let that happen."

Kat's father was obviously angry and I needed to be careful with my answer. It really wasn't my job to watch out for his daughter. It may have been implied, but no one actually told me that was what I was supposed to do. Still I didn't want to say anything that would stoke his anger. And I didn't want to place the blame on Kat.

I decided to take one for the team.

"You're right. I should have been with her and I should have been the one to hit the guy. When she told me to stay in the motorhome while she went in to get food, I should have said, 'No,' and gone in with her. But I didn't. It was my fault. I just didn't think she could get into much trouble inside a Walmart. I was wrong.

"In her defense, your daughter probably saved that little girl's life. The store's video clearly shows that—"

Kat's father interrupted me. "There's a video?"

"Yes sir, there is. The store has security cameras all over the place and they record everything. According to the police, the video shows your daughter was justified in doing what she did."

Kat's father sounded relieved. "That's good to hear. But what about the video? Who has copies?"

I thought for a moment. "The police. They have a copy. They got it from the store manager. The store has the original."

"Anyone else?"

That was a good question, one I didn't know the answer to. I wasn't going to lie, so I told him the truth.

"I don't know if there are other copies. We left town as soon as the police said there were no charges. I didn't think it was wise for us to hang around."

I waited for his reply. For a few seconds he said nothing. I was starting to worry, but then he said, "Walker, I'm not going to hold this one against you. But if something like this happens again when she's with you, you and I are going to have a problem. You understand?"

"Yes sir, I understand."

"Good. Just so we're clear, when she's with you, you're responsible for her. I'm going to hold you to that."

He ended the call.

I turned and handed the phone back to Kat.

"What'd he say?"

I thought about it before I answered. I didn't want say anything that might anger Kat. But she needed to know what her father had said. Her knowing might make my life easier.

"He said when I'm with you, you're my responsibility. If you do something that gets you hurt or in trouble, I'm going to be one who has to pay the price. He was very clear about that."

Kat smiled. "So, you're going to be responsible for all the trouble I get into. That means you're going to have to follow me around like a puppy dog and make sure I don't mess up. That'll make things real interesting."

She turned to Devin. "We'll have to see what kind of trouble we can get into and whether Walker here can stop us. Where should we start?"

Devin smiled. "How about we turn on the TV? See if we made the local news."

Kat turned to me. "You heard her, turn on the TV."

I didn't want to watch TV. It'd been a long day and I just wanted to go to bed. But if the girls had made the local news, it was probably a good idea for us to know about it. I grabbed the remote.

Devin said, "Go to channel forty-nine. If it's on the news, it'll be there."

I tuned to forty-nine and waited.

The ten o'clock news had just started. The lead story was, "Kidnapping thwarted at Walmart."

We listened as the news babe came on and delivered the story. According to her, a recently released sex offender attempted to kidnap a twelve-year-old girl from the Perry Walmart store. The kidnapping was thwarted when an alert shopper saw what was happening and took action.

"The good Samaritan picked up an iron skillet and struck the kidnapper on the head, knocking him out. The store security system recorded the entire attack. After viewing the video, the police said it clearly shows how the actions of the heroic shopper stopped a kidnapping.

"The child's mother, who was shopping in a different part of the store when the event took place, said the woman who stopped the kidnapper should be hailed as a hero. The police agreed.

"Had it not been for the quick action of this woman, the kidnapper might have succeeded. The man, Daniel J. Lamonia, 36, was taken to a nearby hospital and will be arrested and held without bail.

"The names of the child as well as the woman who saved her have not been released. The police said the shopper was justified in her action and no charges will be filed against her."

Accompanying the news report were several images, including a Google map showing the store location, a photo of the Walmart parking lot, a police photo of the kidnapper, and a photo of the Walmart kitchen department with a close-up of several skillets hanging on a rack.

When the story was over, I muted the TV and said, "Congratulations. You made the evening news. They say you're a hero. Too bad no one except for us will know it was you."

Actually, I was pretty happy they didn't mention Kat's name and didn't show the video of the attack. If they had, Kat's father would be calling me again.

I turned the TV off. "Time to go to bed. You and Devin are sleeping out here on the couch. There are pillows and sheets in the overhead bin. I'm going to walk to the bathhouse and when I get back, it's going to be lights out."

I helped fold the couch out into a bed then grabbed a flashlight and headed outside. With three of us in the motorhome for the night, I figured giving them the bathroom while I was out was probably the safe way to go.

When I returned, Devin was curled up on the couch covered by a sheet. Bob was beside her. I assumed Kat was still in the bathroom, getting ready for bed.

But I was wrong.

Chapter Twenty-three

Kat wasn't in the bathroom. She was in my bed. It looked like she was naked. I couldn't tell for sure because she'd covered herself from the chest down with a sheet, leaving only her bare shoulders and head visible. She was pretending to sleep, but I wasn't buying it.

"You can't sleep in here."

She didn't respond.

"Kat, you're not sleeping in here. You need to get up and get on the couch with Devin."

Again, no response.

I reached over to tap her on the shoulder. To do this, I had to lean far across the bed, which made what happened next not my fault.

Just as I was about to touch her, she opened her eyes, grabbed my hand and pulled. I was already off balance and her pull was all that was needed to tip me into the bed next to her. My head landed next to hers.

She leaned over and whispered. "I'm sleeping in here with you tonight. There's nothing you can say or do that's going to change that. You might as well get used to it."

I started to roll away from her, but she still had my hand. "Walker, listen to me. I'm doing this to protect you. If I'm not here in bed with you, Devin will be. She'll wait until she thinks I'm asleep then she'll sneak in here and try to have her way.

"You don't want that to happen. It'll be trouble with a capital T. So do yourself a favor, lock the door, turn off the lights and get in bed. And just in case you haven't figured it out, I'm naked. That's the way I sleep. When I get cold tonight, I'm going to need someone to cuddle with. It's going to be you."

She's naked and she wants to cuddle? Normally I'd look forward to spending the night with a naked woman, especially one as good looking as Kat. But having just spoken with her father, I wasn't sure it would be in my best interest to sleep with his daughter.

On the other hand, the only other place for me to sleep inside the motorhome would be on the couch next to Devin. That too could be trouble. What I really needed was a bigger motorhome. One with more beds. Or fewer women.

I pulled away from Kat and got up out of bed. I went up front, locked all the doors and turned off the lights. I checked Bob's food and water in the bathroom and then reluctantly returned to my bedroom where Kat was no longer pretending to sleep. She was lying on her side, waiting for my return.

She patted the empty space beside her and said, "Take your clothes off and get in here with me."

It was an offer I couldn't refuse.

I turned off the nightlight, dropped my pants, pulled off my shirt and crawled in bed beside her. She snuggled up against me and whispered, "Relax. You don't have to do anything. Just enjoy my company."

When I woke the next morning, the underwear I was wearing when I crawled into bed the night before was nowhere to be found. Kat was in the bed beside me, snoring softly.

Hearing Devin rattling pans in the kitchen reminded me we weren't alone in the motorhome. I tried to ease out of bed without disturbing Kat, but as soon as I moved, she rolled over and put her arm over my chest. "Where do you think you're going?"

I gently lifted her arm. "To the bathroom, I've got to pee."

She giggled. "Come back and see me when you get done. We've got some unfinished business to take care of."

She rolled onto her side, giving me a chance to escape. I slid out of bed, found my shorts on the floor and pulled them on. I grabbed my shirt and headed toward the bathroom.

As soon as I stepped into the hall, Devin was on me. She was wearing a T-shirt and nothing else. She came up and put her hand on my chest. "You hungry? 'Cause I've got something for you. I think you'll like it."

It didn't sound like she was talking about breakfast, but I let it slide. It was too early in the day to try to parse her meaning. I stumbled back and pushed my way into the bathroom. For a moment, I thought Devin was going to follow me. I was relieved when she didn't.

I took care of business and washed my hands. I brushed my teeth and tried to make myself presentable. Opening the bathroom door, I found Kat standing in her black panties and matching bra. She had a wicked smile on her face. "I thought you were coming back to bed. I waited for you, but you didn't come. That means you owe me one. I plan to collect tonight."

I didn't know how to reply, so I kissed her gently on the forehead and moved out of her way. She stepped into the bathroom and when she closed the door behind her, I headed to the kitchen. Devin was waiting for me. She had heard what Kat had said.

"You need to be careful around her. Her daddy won't like it if he finds out you two have been fooling around."

She turned to the stove and pointed at the dozen eggs on the counter. "How do you want 'em?"

Before I could answer she said, "I hope you like scrambled because that's what you're getting."

"Scrambled sounds good. Anything I can do to help you?"

She turned to face me. "Yes, you can give me a hug. I kind of feel left out."

She stepped in close and wrapped her arms around me. Then she stood on her tiptoes and kissed me on the lips.

Not wanting Kat to catch us, I pulled back and whispered, "Are you crazy? What if Kat sees you kissing me? You can't do this."

She smiled. "I can do whatever I want. And I could tell you liked it. So don't play high and mighty with me."

She took a step back, winked and cracked two eggs into the iron skillet she and Kat had bought at Walmart the day before.

I had a feeling that before this trip was over the skillet might be used for more than cooking.

Chapter Twenty-four

After breakfast I took a walk while Kat and Devin showered and dressed. I didn't want to be in the motorhome alone with either of them while the other was in the bathroom or otherwise occupied. I was afraid Devin would try to 'one up' Kat or Kat would want to collect on what she said I owed her from the night before.

It was beginning to feel like it was some sort of contest between the two girls and I was the prize. It was the kind of contest most men dream about, having two beautiful women fighting over him. But not so much when both of them were borderline crazy and had fathers known to deal in pain.

Still, no matter my misgivings on the contest, it was going to be difficult to resist the temptation to play along, especially since, during our walk night before, Kat had made a point of telling me to 'play along'.

I didn't want to disappoint her, and in light of the previous night's activities, it sounded like 'playing along' had some major benefits.

I'd been out walking for twenty minutes. Plenty of time for the girls to get ready to hit the road again. When I got back to the motorhome, they were both on the couch. Bob was curled up between them. Devin had made up the bed and put away the sheets and pillowcases. The kitchen dishes had been washed and put up and it looked like both girls were ready for travel. I was glad to see it. We needed to cover a lot miles before the day was over.

I looked at Kat and asked, "What's the plan?"

She looked at Devin and they nodded liked they had agreed to something while I was outside on my walk. I got the distinct feeling that maybe I should have stayed inside and been a part of whatever they had discussed. But I hadn't, so my vote apparently didn't count.

"We're going to Devin's place in Niceville to pick up the package for my father. To keep it interesting, we're going to take the long way, following the shore all the way to Apalachicola. We'll eat lunch there at a burger place I know. Then we'll stay on 98 through Mexico Beach. When we get to Panama City, we'll head north to Niceville.

"If all goes well, we'll get to Devin's place around three. And since you don't know the way, I'll be driving."

Normally, I wouldn't have let her drive. It's my motorhome and I like driving it. But I'd promised to help her learn to drive a motorhome and she needed more time behind the wheel. Today's easy drive on Florida's back roads might satisfy her.

"Okay, you can drive. But before you do, you need to know how to break camp. That means you have to go outside with me and unhook everything."

I went to the side door and held it open for her, letting her go out first. Outside, I led her to the motorhome's utility compartment and pointed at the hoses and cables that tethered us to the campground.

"First thing, disconnect from shore power. Coil up the power cord and put it in the storage compartment. Do the same with the TV cable then turn off the water at the tap, disconnect the hose, and put it in the compartment."

I expected her to complain as I stood back and did nothing, but she didn't. Instead, she followed my instructions and took care to do it right. When she was done, she turned to me and said, "That was easy. Nothing to it."

"Glad you feel that way because now you get to dump the holding tanks. The showers you and Devin took this morning probably filled them up."

I pointed to the open storage compartment. "There's a pair of rubber gloves in there. You'll want to put them on."

She picked up the gloves. "You sure we need to dump the tanks? Maybe we should wait and do it tomorrow."

"No, we need to do it today. If we don't, there's a good chance that when you flush the toilet, it'll back up on the floor. You probably don't want that. So put the gloves on, okay?"

She didn't argue. She put the gloves on and held her hands high so I could see she was wearing them. "Happy?"

I smiled. "I will be. Just as soon as you dump the tanks."

I pointed at the brown sewer hose in the storage compartment. "Grab the hose and put the pointy end in the hole in the ground over there.

"Then pull the cap off the sewer pipe on the motorhome and connect the hose to it. Don't stand too close when you pull the cap. There might be some leakage."

Again, I expected Kat to complain, but, like before, she didn't. In fact, she acted like she knew what she was doing. More than likely, she'd learned how to do this back when she and Devin were buying and selling travel trailers. They'd have had the same kind of sewer hookup.

When she had the hoses connected, she pulled the handle labeled, "Black tank." We heard the distinctive sound of lumpy water flowing from the motorhome holding tank through the sewer hose into the campground's sewage tank.

When the lumpy water noise subsided, Kat pulled the handle labeled "Gray tank" and again we heard a rush of water going through the sewer hose into the underground tank. After the water noise stopped, she closed both handles, disconnected the sewer hose from the motorhome and held it up so that any remaining sewage would drain off into the underground tank.

Having completed the task, she placed end caps on the hose and stored it in the utility compartment along with the rubber gloves she'd been wearing. She used the campground water to rise off her hands.

"Okay boss, how'd I do?"

She'd done a good job and there was no reason not to tell her. "You did good, especially for someone who supposedly didn't know how to do this."

She smiled. "Let's go inside and finish up."

Chapter Twenty-five

Back inside, I held Bob while Kat pushed the button to bring in the slide room. I watched as she checked to make sure all the cabinets and drawers were securely closed and anything that could move while we were going down the road was put away.

When she was done, I did a quick walk through to make sure she hadn't missed anything. She had. The sliding bathroom door. It needed to be locked in the open position so it wouldn't slide with a guillotine like force at each corner or curve in the road. With Bob's food and litter in the bathroom, it would be tragic if the sliding door caught him midway in.

I didn't fault Kat for not locking the door. It was something I hadn't mentioned and there was no way she would have known if I hadn't told her why it was important. After I explained the logic, she locked the door open and checked to make sure it wouldn't move. She didn't want Bob to get hurt either.

With the bathroom door secure, Kat went back up front and sat in the driver's seat. I took the passenger seat and Devin stayed on the couch with Bob.

Kat got the motorhome started and was careful backing out of our campsite. She took it slow, checking the mirrors and rear view camera to make sure nothing was blocking her way. When she got to the highway, she checked both ways to make sure there was no traffic and then pulled out. Soon we were cruising down US 98 at sixty miles an hour.

The Gulf of Mexico was on our left, pine forests on our right. The road was two lane with very little traffic. The GPS showed it was a straight shot to Apalachicola, thirty five miles ahead.

With Kat driving, I was free to look out the windows and watch the world go by. It was strange to be so close to the waters of the Gulf of Mexico, just thirty feet off to our left, without seeing any commercial buildings or high rises.

It was like the big developers had forgotten that this part of coastal Florida existed. Or maybe the frequent hurricanes scared them off. Whatever the reason, it was nice to be able to see the coast in its natural state with no commercial development.

The only businesses we saw were on the right side of the road, scattered a few miles apart, mostly small mom and pop RV parks set under towering pines with direct access to the Gulf of Mexico. These looked like nice places to spend a few weeks and forget about what was going on in the rest of the world.

It stayed like this almost all the way to Apalachicola. But things changed when we reached the small town of East Point. It sat across the bay from Apalachicola, connected via the John Gorrie Bridge, which rose up and spanned the St Marks and Apalachicola rivers as they flowed into the Gulf of Mexico.

As we topped the bridge, I could see downtown Apalachicola and the oyster boats that made the city famous. Across the street from the boats were small rustic eateries, most serving fresh oysters and whatever else the boats had brought in as the catch of the day.

I looked over at Kat, who was still driving, and asked,

"Are we going to stop in Apalach and eat?"

She shook her head. "No, not unless you really want to. It's too early in the day for oysters. And anyway, I'd rather eat at the Sunset Grill in Saint Joe. It's about twenty minutes down the road. But ask Devin, see what she says."

Devin was still behind us on the couch and probably couldn't hear what we were saying up front. I got up and went back to ask her about lunch. With the motorhome in motion, I had to support myself with the overhead cabinets to keep my balance. When I reached Devin, I plopped down on the couch beside her.

She looked up and said, "You came to see me. Good. I've been lonely back here. What do you have in mind?"

"Lunch. I was thinking maybe we should stop here in Apalach but Kat says we should wait until we get to Saint Joe. I wanted to know what you thought."

Devin took my hand and put it in her lap. "I want to do whatever will make you happy. But in this case I'm going to have to agree with Kat. It'll be hard to park the motorhome on the narrow streets of Apalach. There's more room at the place she's thinking about in Saint Joe."

I nodded. "Okay, it's settled then. We're going to eat in Saint Joe."

I started to get up, but Devin was still holding my hand and didn't let go. "Stay back here with me. It'll give us a chance to get to know each other a little better."

The top three buttons of her shirt were undone and I was pretty sure they weren't like that when we left earlier in the day. I would have noticed. The buttons could have come undone on their own, but it was unlikely. The view was interesting, but I was feeling maybe I shouldn't be looking. Then again, maybe Devin would appreciate it if I mentioned it to her. I started to say something, but Kat called out. "Walker, I need you up here."

Her timing was perfect. It gave me an excuse to walk away from Devin and the trouble I could have easily gotten into. I gently removed my hand from hers and headed back up front.

As soon as I sat in the passenger seat, Kat pointed to a Piggly Wiggly and said, "We could stop there if you want. They have food."

Before I answered, I should have figured out why she thought the question was so important I needed to come back up front. But I didn't. Instead I said, "Piggly Wiggly? I thought you wanted to eat in Saint Joe. I asked Devin and she agreed with you."

Kat looked over at me. "Yeah, I heard what she said. Every bit of it."

She patted my knee. "You might be better off staying up here with me. Might be safer for you."

I felt the same way.

Chapter Twenty-six

Leaving Apalachicola, we stayed on US 98 heading west. The road bordered the coast for about six miles before turning north. The terrain going north was still flat, but our view of the Gulf had been replaced by tall, skinny pine trees. There was almost no traffic on this stretch of road. No high rise hotels, no condos and no theme parks. A constant reminder of why this part of Florida was called the Forgotten Coast. It was basically the same as it had been for the past fifty years. Palm trees and beaches with a smattering of small towns mixed in.

The speed limit was fifty-five and Kat was keeping pretty close to it. I could tell she was enjoying the drive. It would be hard not to. The skies were blue, the road was in good shape and the motorhome was performing well.

She hadn't said much since that morning, other than answering my question about where we were going to eat. But that was typical Kat. She didn't feel like she always needed to pad the silence with her words. She was content to simply say nothing if nothing needed to be said. Whenever she did say something, it was usually important, at least to her. So when she said, "Walker, I really want to buy your motorhome," I knew she was serious.

She'd mentioned this back when we were in Key West, but I wasn't interested in selling. I had no reason to sell. I liked my motorhome. It had everything I needed. It was easy to drive and it was paid for.

I was thinking about this when she said, "I'm serious. I want you to sell me your motorhome. The more I drive it the more I want to buy it. This is the one I want."

I'd been helping her look for a motorhome, but so far she hadn't found any that she really liked. We'd been to several RV lots and walked through at least a hundred different coaches. She'd had a Goldilocks opinion about most of them; they were too small, too big, too old or too expensive.

When we'd walk away from motorhome viewings, she'd almost always say, "I want to buy your motorhome. Sell me yours. It's the one I want."

And every time I'd tell her the same thing. "Kat, mine's not for sale. Everything I own is in it and if I sold it to you, I wouldn't have a place to live."

That usually ended the discussion. But not this time. She smiled and said, "That's what you keep saying. You can't sell it to me because you wouldn't have a place to live. But there's an easy solution to that problem."

She paused and I thought she was about to tell me the easy solution. But instead she pointed ahead and said, "That's where we're going to eat."

She tapped the right turn signal, slowed down, and pulled into a gravel covered parking lot. An old trailer that at one time had been white sat at the back of the lot. A hand painted sign on the front of the trailer said, "Paul Gants Bar-b-que."

An old air conditioner supported by a warped 2×4 hung precariously from the side window. A faded blue awning over the lone window in the front provided shade for those brave enough to step up and order food.

Kat pulled the motorhome to the back of the lot, out of the way of anyone else who might be tempted to pull in.

That was nice of her, but judging by the lack of cars already in the lot, I didn't expect there'd be many joining us. But if they did, there'd be plenty of room for them to park.

I wasn't sure we were at the right place. She'd said earlier we'd be eating at the Sunset Grill. Maybe she'd changed her mind. I decided to ask. "Is this where we're eating?"

She turned and gave me the look. The kind you get when you ask a woman a stupid question. "Yes, this is where we're eating. Unless you don't think your delicate tummy can handle barbeque."

I could tell she was feeling good, she was smiling when she said this and I knew she meant it as a friendly jibe. Still, I didn't want to leave it hanging without a response.

"I like barbeque. I just thought you were more of a salad girl."

She smiled. "Yeah right."

She turned to Devin. "Barbeque okay with you?"

Devin didn't hesitate with her answer. "You bet. Get me one of their pulled pork sandwiches with coleslaw on the side."

Kat turned to me. "I want the same. You go get it and I'll have everything ready when you come back."

Sounded like a plan to me. I grabbed my wallet and reached for the keys to the motorhome. They were still in the ignition and I had to reach across Kat to get them.

She made a face. "You're taking the keys? You don't trust me?"

I knew she was going to ask that and I had an answer ready. "It's not that I don't trust you, I just need the keys so I can unlock the door when I come back in."

I had no intention of locking the door when I left, but I

didn't want to leave the keys in the motorhome. It would be too easy for her to start it up and drive away without me. I grabbed the keys and headed outside.

I walked up to the dusty, white barbeque trailer and stood at the little window next to the menu board. An older woman with red hair slid open the window and asked, "What you having today, honey?"

I ordered three pork sandwiches with coleslaw on the side. I didn't order any drinks because I knew we had cold ones back in the fridge. The woman took my order and said, "Coming right up."

She disappeared into the back of the trailer, presumably to put our order together. While she was doing this, I took a few steps back away from the window. I wanted to see what the motorhome looked like from across the parking lot. It's something you do if you're a guy. You always check out your ride from across the way.

From what I could see, Kat was no longer in the driver's seat, but because the large side windows were tinted, I couldn't see if she or Devin had moved to the kitchen table. If they had, they were probably watching me. I waved just in case.

Behind me, I heard, "Your order's ready."

The woman who'd taken my order was holding two white paper bags. A grease circle was spreading on the bottom half of one of them, probably from the pork sandwiches. I was hoping it wasn't the coleslaw. I'd already paid, so I took the bags and headed back to the motorhome.

Just as I got to it, I heard a loud truck pull into the lot behind me. I turned and saw an older Ford F350 dually pickup, faded white with two grinning monkeys painted on the door. Under it, in faded paint, were the words, "Trailer

Monkeys."

I shook my head and stepped into the motorhome. After putting the bags of food on the kitchen table, I pointed out the window to the truck that had just pulled into the lot.

"Isn't that the guys you were telling me about? The Trailer Monkeys?"

Kat looked out the window. "That's their truck, but it can't be them. No way they'd still be in business all these years. Maybe they sold it to somebody else."

She seemed surprised, but not nearly as much as I thought someone who ran into a long-lost friend after ten years would be. It seemed kind of suspicious this coincidental meet-up, especially after the coincidental meet-up of Devin back in Crystal River.

I probably shouldn't have but I asked her about it. "Kat, tell me you didn't plan this. Tell me you didn't set up a meeting with the Trailer Monkeys. Tell me you pulling into this parking lot just minutes before the Trailer Monkeys pull in is just a coincidence. Tell me it's not something you planned like yesterday's meet up with Devin."

She held up her right hand as if taking an oath. "I promise I didn't plan this. I didn't know they'd be here. I haven't seen or spoken to either of them in years and I sure didn't expect to see them here today."

I turned to Devin, who'd already dug into the bag of food and grabbed one of the sandwiches. I asked her the same thing. "Devin, tell the truth. Did you or Kat plan this ahead of time? Did either of you know the Trailer Monkeys would be here?"

She shook her head. "I don't know about Kat, but I swear I didn't know they'd be here. I thought they'd either be in jail or dead by now."

Kat stood and moved away from the window. "I don't want them to see me. I don't want to talk to them and I don't want them to know I'm here. Maybe we should just leave."

She sounded like she was serious. Like she didn't have anything to do with them showing up and didn't want them to know she was around. I wasn't fully convinced but didn't see a reason to push it, at least not yet. I wanted to eat lunch, so I said, "Kat, they can't see you through the tinted windows, so let's just sit here and eat our lunch. We can watch and see what they do."

She peeked out the window. "Are you sure they can't see us?"

"I'm sure. The only way they're going to see you is if you walk over there and talk to them."

"Well, I'm not doing that."

Convinced they couldn't see her though the dark tinted glass she sat down at the table and grabbed a sandwich. I did the same.

We watched out the window as we ate. The pork sandwich was good, maybe the best barbeque I'd had while on the road. Certainly the best I'd had in the company of two good looking women.

While we watched, a man, about thirty-five with a dark tan and wearing dusty clothes, got out on the driver's side of the truck and walked over to the trailer to place his order.

Kat nodded. "That's Pico."

No one else got out of the truck and it didn't look like anyone else was in it. Pico placed his order and went back to the truck to wait. He pulled out his phone and made a call. After speaking a few words, he hung up.

A few minutes later, the woman at the order window

waved at him, letting him know his food was ready. As he walked over to pick it up, another car pulled into the lot. An older Chevy. Dark blue Monte Carlo with heavily tinted windows, riding on chrome wheels. Three men came out of the car and headed for Pico. He didn't see them coming. One of the men grabbed him from behind and held him while another started punching him.

The third man walked back to the Monte Carlo, grabbed what looked like a tire iron and headed back toward Pico. His intentions didn't look good.

Chapter Twenty-seven

I didn't know Pico and didn't care what he'd done to make the three men mad enough to want to give him a beating. All I knew was it wasn't a fair fight and I wasn't going to sit by and do nothing.

Almost all motorhomes come with a fire extinguisher. Small, red ones usually strapped to the wall near the side door. Mine was metal and weighed about nine pounds. I grabbed it and headed outside. I could see the guys still pounding on Pico. It wasn't a pretty sight.

I pulled the pin on the extinguisher and headed in their direction. They were too busy throwing punches to hear me come up behind them. When I got three feet away, I aimed the extinguisher and squeezed the handle. A blast of slippery white foam quickly covered the backs of the two men throwing the punches.

They stopped working on Pico and turned to face me.

"What the hell you doing?" the larger of the two men asked.

"Stopping a fight."

"The hell you are. You just signed up for a beating of your own."

He raised both fists and moved quickly toward me.

I flipped the extinguisher over, flat bottom facing out. When the man got within striking distance, I swung the extinguisher like a battering ram and caught him just below his ribcage, in the soft part of his belly.

The blow caught him by surprise, knocking the wind out of him and causing him to lose his balance. As he struggled to stay upright, I flipped the extinguisher over, pointed the nozzle at his face and squeezed the handle. The blast of white foam blanketed his eyes, nose and mouth. Temporarily blinded, he stumbled and fell to the ground.

I turned my attention to his partner. He had stood by and watched when the first man came at me. He probably thought his larger friend would have no problem taking me out. But he was wrong. Now it was his turn to step in and try to finish me off. He wouldn't be using his fists though. He was still holding the tire iron he'd gotten out of the car. It looked like he planned to use it on me.

He held it high and rushed toward me. It looked like he was planning to bring the iron down on my head. I had a different plan.

When he swung the iron, I brought the extinguisher up and blocked the blow. Then, with the nozzle level with his face, I squeezed the handle. The blast of pressurized foam coated his face like icing on a cake. Like his partner, it temporarily blinded him. He wiped at his eyes with his free hand, still holding the tire iron in the other. I hated to hit a man who wasn't looking, but I needed to end this quickly. I flipped the extinguisher over and brought it down on his shoulder with enough force to take him to the ground.

Two down, one to go.

I turned to the man holding Pico. He had watched me take on his two buddies and now it was his turn. But he'd decided to become a pacifist. He pushed Pico away, raised both hands and said, "It's cool. I'm leaving."

He turned and made a move for his car, but Pico wasn't

having any of it. He grabbed the man from behind, spun him around and landed a solid blow to the side of his head. The man stumbled a few steps backwards then fell to the ground. He made no effort to get up.

Pico turned to me, grunted a thanks and limped back to his truck. He reached inside and came out with what looked like a long handled ice pick. I was afraid he was going to use it on the guy on the ground. But he didn't. He walked over to the Monte Carlo and shoved the ice pick into the driver's side front tire. Air hissed out as the tire went flat. He pulled the ice pick out, walked to the back of the car and used the pick again. With two tires going flat, Pico looked in my direction and nodded. Then he walked back to his truck and drove off.

The three men who had attacked him were still on the ground. Two were covered in sticky white foam, bits of dirt and gravel from the ground stuck to them. The man Pico had punched was also on the ground. He didn't seem to be in much of a hurry to get up.

It hadn't started out as a fair fight. It hadn't ended that way either. When it comes to fighting, there's no such thing as fair. There are only winners and losers.

The three men on the ground were the losers. I didn't wait around to tell them that. I walked back to the motorhome, dusting myself off on the way. Kat met me at the door. I tossed her the keys and said, "We need to leave. You drive."

The parking lot had two entrances, one on the front where it bordered US 98, and one on the back, which led to a side street. I pointed to the one at the back and said, "Go out that way. Turn right. Take the first two lefts. That should get us back to the highway. Then head west."

I didn't wait to see if she had any questions. I headed to the back to wash up. Devin was still sitting at the kitchen table, watching the three men on the ground in the parking lot. As I passed her, I asked, "Did they see me get in the motorhome? Do they know what we're driving?"

She shook her head. "I don't think they saw you coming or going. You were like a ninja. When the fight started, you weren't there. And then you were. When it was over, you were gone.

"It was just you and them, no witnesses. Except for Pico. And he's not going to tell anyone."

"Good. We don't need any trouble from this."

Kat had started the motorhome and it lurched forward when she put it in gear. I grabbed the overhead compartment to keep from falling on Devin. I held tight while Kat got us out of the parking lot. When I saw her take a right, I made my way to the bathroom.

It didn't take long to wash the foam from my hands and wipe the dust off my face. When I came out, I could see that Kat had us back on 98 and we were going in the right direction—heading west, away from Saint Joe and the three men in the parking lot.

With the two flat tires, it would be a while before they could come after us. I was hoping they didn't know what we were in or what direction we were going. That'd make our lives a lot easier. When I came back up front, Devin was still sitting at the kitchen table. My uneaten sandwich where I had left it.

I sat down and took a bite.

Devin was sitting across from me, wide eyed. "That was the most amazing thing I've ever seen. You took care of all three of them in less than a minute. You walked away without a scratch. Here I was thinking you were some kind of wimp. Boy, was I wrong. You didn't hesitate to mix it up with them. I gotta tell you, I'm impressed.

"One question though. Did you think you hurt them? Will they need to go to the hospital?"

I shook my head. "They're not hurt. The foam from the extinguisher is mostly wet baking soda. It's safe. They'll wash it off and be okay."

Devin seemed relieved. "Good. I wanted them to leave Pico alone, but didn't want to see them get hurt."

She called up to Kat. "Why didn't you tell me Walker was a ninja with super powers?"

Chapter Twenty-eight

Devin was still sitting across from me as I was finishing off my sandwich. She was excited about the fight and wanted to talk about it.

"Walker, I've seen a lot of fights but never one that ended so quickly. Most of the time, the guys punch each other and then roll around on the ground until they get tired and somebody quits.

"But it was different with you. You went out there against three guys and ended it in less than a minute. That's what's really amazing. You took out those guys and didn't break a sweat."

I had listened to her long enough. It was time to shut her down. "Devin, I don't like fighting. I'll avoid a fight if there is any way I can. But if I can't, I fight and do whatever it takes to end it quickly. If I can do it without hurting the other guy, that's even better.

"That fight today, those guys will walk away without any broken bones. Maybe a few bruises, but no permanent damage. That's the only thing I feel good about. The rest I'd rather forget. So, if you don't mind, let's not talk about it anymore. Okay?"

Kat was still driving. She'd gotten us back on 98 and we were heading west toward Panama City. We'd been on the road about fifteen minutes when she called out, "Walker, I need some help up here."

She was up front alone; Devin and I were still at the kitchen table. I got up and walked to the front to see what she wanted. "What do you need?"

She pointed at the dark gray clouds moving in from the gulf off to our left. "I think we're heading into a storm. The wind is starting to push me all over the road. If it comes up a storm, I don't want to be driving."

The thing about a motorhome is you have to be careful when there's a lot of wind, especially when the wind is coming in from the side. A sudden gust can push the motorhome off the road or into oncoming traffic. To compensate, you have to be ready to steer into the wind just enough to keep the front of the coach pointed in the right direction. But if the wind stops, you have to straighten the wheel to keep it out of the ditch.

In the afternoon storms that are common in Florida in the summer, winds can gust up over fifty miles an hour, making it dangerous to be on a narrow road in a high profile vehicle like a motorhome. For a new driver like Kat, it can be terrifying.

With the storm quickly approaching, I said, "Pull over the first place you see with enough room to park."

We were just getting into the small town of Mexico beach. The narrow strip of white sand of the Gulf of Mexico was on our left, small shops and stilt houses on our right. Kat slowed and started looking for a place to pull over.

Normally, we'd pull into the nearest mall or superstore parking lot. These always had enough room to park a motorhome. But there weren't any malls or superstores on the Forgotten Coast, certainly none in the small town of Mexico Beach. The few parking spaces available were designed for cars and most were already taken.

The wind had picked up and it was starting to rain. The road was getting slick and Kat was getting nervous. To make matters worse, she was having a hard time finding the switch to turn on the windshield wipers.

She had one hand on the steering wheel, the other fumbling with the wiper switch when a strong gust of wind hit us broadside. The force pushed the right front tire off the pavement. A few more feet and we would be in the ditch. Kat reacted quickly. She instinctively lifted off the gas and steered to the left, bringing us back on the road. But the close call had shaken her. She was ready to call it quits. But there was nowhere to park.

Looking ahead, I saw a sign on our right that said, "Public Boat Launch." Just beyond it was a small road. I pointed and said, "Turn off there."

Kat didn't bother with the turn signal; she kept both hands firmly on the wheel, fighting the wind. She tapped the brakes several times in a row, slowing the motorhome and alerting cars behind us that something was up. She'd gotten our speed down to under ten miles per hour when she took the boat ramp turn-off. The road was narrow, dirt packed and filled with potholes. She followed it to the mostly empty parking lot and found a place near the edge to park.

After killing the motor, she looked at me and said, "That was scary."

I nodded. "Yeah, I know. But you did good. You saw a storm coming and you started looking for a safe place to park. That's the right thing to do. When you see a storm, park it.

"Now that we're parked, we can start the generator, run the air conditioner and bide our time until it blows over. If it doesn't blow over, we can spend the night here. We have everything we need."

Kat nodded but I could tell she was still shaken. She handed me the keys and said, "You can drive the rest of the way."

I started to say something, but she shook her head. As far as she was concerned, she was done. She didn't want to hear any more about it. She got up out of the driver's seat and walked back to the bathroom, closing the door behind her. I waited a minute then went back and took a seat on the couch beside Devin. I didn't expect her to say anything about Kat's driving, and she didn't.

As we sat there, we could hear a heavy band of rain marching across the parking lot, heading in our direction. It was followed by a gust of wind stronger than the one that had almost pushed us off the road. Even though we were parked, the wind rocked the motorhome. I could see the steering wheel move on its own, responding to the force of the wind on the tires. If either Kat or I were still driving in a storm of this magnitude, I don't know if we could have kept it on the road.

Kat was coming back up front when the first clap of thunder hit. It surprised her and she let out a yelp, just as Bob scooted by, brushing her leg. He headed straight for my lap, leaping from the floor onto the couch where I was sitting. He stayed just long enough for me to stroke his back.

I told him it was just a storm, nothing to worry about, but I sensed he didn't believe me. At the second clap of thunder, he tore out of my lap and headed to his safe space in the closet in my bedroom.

I had a feeling if there had been enough room in the closet Kat would have joined him there. Instead, she walked over to the couch and reached out to me with her hand.

"Come with me," she whispered.

I stood and followed her back to the bedroom. She lay down on the bed and said, "Hold me."

I could tell she was stressed, probably from the drive or maybe seeing her friend Pico being attacked in the barbeque parking lot. Either way, I was happy to help her. I lay down beside her and she snuggled up against me.

The rain was coming down harder, the thunder rattled the coach's windows and the wind gusts continued to rock us side-to-side. It had gotten eerily dark outside. There was no doubt we were in the middle of a serious storm.

I could have gotten up and used my phone to check the weather. I had a radar app and could have used it to show Kat it would soon be over. But I didn't. I liked being in the bed beside her and didn't see any reason to get up. We would wait out the storm together.

Devin was stretched out on the couch. She was alone but I got a feeling she was used to it. She hadn't complained when Kat had come for me, and hadn't bothered to come back and join us. I don't know what I would have done if she had.

The storm lasted another twenty minutes. It ended with the same suddenness with which it had begun. It was as if someone had turned off the rain switch. The percussive noise of the heavy raindrops on the roof ended, replaced by the ticking sound of the motorhome's metal skin being warmed by the returning sun.

Kat had rolled over and was facing the window. The sun coming in through the blinds cast a horizontal pattern of dark and light lines on her face. Her eyes were closed and her breathing slow and steady. I didn't want to wake her, but we still had miles to go to get to Devin's place. It was there that the package we were supposed to pick up and take back to Kat's father was located.

The sooner we got the package the sooner we could be on our way back home. I started to get up out of bed, but Kat stirred. She turned and whispered, "Thanks for helping Pico back there. I'm glad you didn't get hurt."

Chapter Twenty-nine

Kat held on to the front of my shirt, keeping me in the bed beside her. She'd just thanked me for helping Pico. I didn't know how to respond so I said nothing.

She waited a moment then asked, "Do you think those guys will be coming after us?"

It didn't sound like she was asking the question out of fear. More likely, she just wanted to know whether we should be prepared or not.

I'd already thought about it and knew what to say. "I'm pretty sure they'll think I was with Pico, riding in the truck with him. Or they'll think I was one of his friends driving by and saw what was happening and decided to help out.

"I don't think they saw me go back in the motorhome. They won't know what we're driving. Won't know what to look for. Even if they did, they wouldn't know which direction we were going when we left. They don't have our plate number and can't use it to track us down. So I doubt they'll be able to find us. But if they do, it's only me they're after. You and Devin will be safe."

She moved closer and whispered, "I hope you're right."

She kissed me lightly on the cheek. "Time to get up. We got miles to go before the day is over."

I took the hint and rolled out of bed. She followed, pushing me toward the front of the coach. Devin was still stretched out on the couch, sleeping or pretending to. Bob was tucked in beside her.

Kat tapped me on the shoulder and whispered, "Take a picture of them sleeping together."

Before I could get to my phone, Devin opened her eyes. "Don't bother, I'm awake. I've been lying here listening to you two back there on the bed. Couldn't hear what you were saying but it sure sounded hot and steamy to me."

She sat up and straightened her shirt. There was a crease down the side of her face that matched the seam around the edge of the couch. That, along with her tousled hair, meant she probably had been sleeping and not just pretending.

Kat sat down on the couch beside Devin and started petting Bob. He responded by purring loudly. While the girls stayed on the couch and cooed over Bob, I checked the windows and doors looking for leaks. In a heavy rain like the one we'd just been through, leaks can be a problem. In a motorhome, it's best to catch them early before they cause mold and damage to the wood framing.

I didn't find any leaks, but did see a lot of debris on the outside of the windows. Mostly small bits of broken palm fronds that had been blown by the strong winds of the storm. I didn't bother to go outside and brush these away. I knew as soon as we got back on the road they would blow away on their own.

I started the motorhome so the girls would know we were getting ready to leave. Kat came up front and sat down in the passenger seat. She buckled her seat belt and said, "I'm ready, as long as you're driving."

I was happy to see her back up front with me. It might mean she was getting her confidence back.

Before pulling away, I looked behind for Devin. I didn't want to drive off with her standing in the aisle or using the bathroom. It wouldn't be polite or safe. I needn't have worried; she was sitting on the couch, ready to go. I put the motorhome in gear and slowly made my way through the now deeply puddled parking lot. When we reached the highway, I pulled out and headed west toward Panama City.

I set the cruise control to fifty-five and drove. Like most of the roads on Florida's Forgotten Coast, this section was a long stretch of two lane highway with nothing but pine forests on either side. Almost no businesses, no homes, no traffic. It was like that all the way to the light at Tyndall Air Force Base on the outskirts of Panama City. There the road divided into four lanes and stayed that way through the city. On my way out of town, the GPS said to get off US 98 and head north on 77. I started to make the turn but Kat said, "Stay on 98. It's a better road."

She knew the area better than I did so I let her override the GPS. I was glad I did as it gave me a chance to drive the outskirts of several beach towns including Seaside, Grayton, and Miramar.

As we approached Destin, Kat had me turn north on 293 and take the toll bridge across the bay. We kept going until we hit state road 20, which led us into downtown Niceville, Devin's home base.

She was still in the back on the couch. I now needed her up front with me. At the first stoplight in Niceville, I called out to her. "Devin, I need you here. You've got to show us the way."

She came up front, changed places with Kat and started giving me directions. "Stay on 20 until you see the Chick-fil-a. When you get to it, turn left on Wise Avenue. Stay on Wise until you get to Dreamland. That's where I live."

"Dreamland? You live in a place called Dreamland? Isn't

that what Michael Jackson called his place?"

She shook her head. "No, his was called Neverland. Mine is called Dreamland. It's not anything like Neverland. You'll see."

No doubt I would. Still, it was kind of funny to think that Devin lived in a place called Dreamland in Niceville. It sounded like something you'd expect see in a Disney movie. The lonely girl from Dreamland meets her handsome prince in Niceville. Hollywood would love it.

I stayed on twenty until I got to the Chick-fil-a then took a left onto Wise street. I stayed on it until the pavement turned to crushed oyster shells – Florida's version of a dirt road. It wasn't the kind of road I envisioned leading to Dreamland. It sure wouldn't be that way in the movie.

We crunched down the oyster shell road for about a mile until we reached a small, hand painted sign on the right that read, "Dreamland Rentals."

Behind the sign stood a row of vintage mobile homes and travel trailers. Older model cars and trucks were parked haphazardly on the grass in front of the homes. The place was far from what I'd envisioned. Instead of being Dreamland, it was more like Dumpland.

"Is this the place?" I asked.

Devin nodded. "This is it. Mine is the fourth trailer on the right."

I turned onto the narrow driveway and drove slowly past the first three trailers. When we reached the fourth driveway, Devin said, "Stop. It isn't here!"

Chapter Thirty

"What do you mean it isn't here?"

Devin pointed at the concrete slab at the end of the short driveway. "It's supposed to be right there. That's my site. But it's not. My trailer is gone."

A white Ford OJ vintage Bronco was parked next to the concrete pad. A set of wooden steps led up to nothing but air. If there had been a trailer there, it was gone now.

"Do you think they moved it to another spot here in Dreamland?"

Devin shook her head. "No, that's not likely. No one would move my trailer without asking me first. They know better. The manager's office is down at the end of the road. Let's go talk to him."

We drove to where the road stopped in front of a 1950s mobile home. It had an art deco look to it and the word 'Spartan' in faded chrome over the door.

The yard in front, defined by a short, white picket fence, was well kept. A walkway made of stepping stones led to the door. A ship's bell served as the doorbell. Devin rang it and followed up with a loud knock in case the manager didn't hear the bell. Kat and I were still out in the motorhome, and we could hear it loud and clear. Apparently the manager had heard it as well. He cracked open the door, looked out and growled, "What do you want?"

The man looked to be in his seventies, short, as some

older men are, but fit. A thick crop of snow-white hair, Clark Kent glasses, a white button up shirt, short pants and house slippers.

He looked at Devin, trying to figure out if he knew her. If he did, it didn't come to him. He saw our motorhome out in the street and said, "We're full up. No vacancies."

As he started to close the door, Devin stopped him. "Mister Parker, it's me. Devin, from number four. I've been renting from you for three years. I'm in the Airstream up near the road."

He looked at her for a moment then appeared to recognize who she was. His mood lightened and he smiled. "Miss McSweeney. What can I do for you today?"

"Do you know who moved my trailer? It's gone."

The old man nodded. "I know it's gone. I saw them move it yesterday. You sold it, right?"

Devin looked over her shoulder to make sure we heard what he'd said. Then she looked back at the manager. "I didn't sell it. What makes you think I did?"

"That's what they told me."

"Who? Who told you I sold it?"

"The men who took it. They came yesterday and started unhooking everything. I went over and talked to them and they said you bought a new trailer and sold them your old one. They even had a bill of sale.

"They stayed until the trailer movers showed up and hauled it away. They was a real professional lot. Took them less than twenty minutes to hook it up and go.

He tipped his glasses down and looked out at us in the motorhome. "Is that your new trailer out there?"

Devin shook her head. "Mister Parker, I didn't buy a new

trailer and I didn't sell my old one. Those guys were stealing it."

The old man looked confused. "They showed me a bill of sale. They said you sold them your trailer. Didn't look like they were stealing it to me."

Devin looked away from the manager and signaled for me to join her. I got out of the motorhome and walked to where they were standing.

"Mister Parker, this is Walker. He's a friend of mine. There was something inside my trailer I was supposed to give him. Did you notice if the guys took anything out of it before they moved it?"

The manager shook his head. "Far as I know, they didn't go inside. Don't think they had a key. They just waited outside until the tow truck came. Then they left, following as it was being towed down the road."

"You say they showed you a bill of sale? Was my name on it?"

The manager hesitated then said, "I didn't have my glasses so I couldn't really make out what it said. It did look like a bill of sale, but I couldn't make out the names on it."

"Any chance you got the plate number of the guys who took it?"

"No, I didn't have any reason to. Even if I did, without my glasses I wouldn't have been able to see it clear enough to read."

Devin took a deep breath. "At least they didn't take my truck. Will it be okay if we park the motorhome in my spot until I get my trailer back?"

"Sure. Your rent's paid up so you got every right to park it there."

Devin thanked the manager and we started walking back to the motorhome. We'd taken about three steps when the manager called out. "I just remembered something. That truck that hauled your trailer away, it had monkeys painted on the door."

Devin wheeled around. "Are you sure?"

"I'm positive. It had monkeys on the door. Grinning monkeys. I'm sure of that. Had some writing below, but I couldn't make it out."

"Mister Parker, you did good. We know who owns that truck. I'll give them a call and find out what's going on."

She started to walk away but I stopped her. I had a question for the manager. "Mister Parker, what were the other men driving? The guys who showed you the bill of sale. What kind of car were they in?"

He looked up to the sky like maybe the answer was in the heavens. I didn't think he was having any luck finding it there because it was taking so long. But finally a smile spread across his face. "It was dark blue. Maybe a Chevy. I'm not positive about that. Today's cars all look alike. Too much wind tunnel testing if you ask me. No way to tell them apart. But I think it was a Chevy. Dark blue. Maybe a Monte Carlo."

Devin smiled. "Mister Parker, that really helps. If you remember anything else, give me a call. You still have my number on file?"

He nodded. "Sure do. I'll call you if I think of anything. I'm real sorry someone took your trailer."

We walked back to the motorhome. Kat was inside and had heard most of what had been said. She had her phone out. "You want me to call them? Squally and Pico? See what they know?"

Devin shook her head. "No, don't call them. Not yet. We don't want to spook them. If they knew it was my Airstream, they wouldn't have taken it. They'd be afraid my dad would send a crew down and skin them alive. If we call them and they have it, they might deny it and try to get rid of it. We don't want that to happen."

Kat put her phone away. "Okay, I won't call them. But what do we do?"

They both looked at me.

Chapter Thirty-one

I don't know why they thought I'd have the answer. I didn't. But I figured if we talked it out, maybe the answer would come to us—or at least part of it.

"Here's what we know. The Trailer Monkeys hauled off Devin's trailer some time yesterday afternoon. There's no doubt about that. And it looks like guys in a blue Chevy hired them to do it. Again, there's no doubt about that.

"It could be the guys in the blue Chevy are the same ones we had a run-in with at the barbeque joint. We know they had a beef with Pico about something and it could have been about the trailer. But that's just a guess.

"We don't know where the Monkeys took the trailer, but we do know that Pico was in Saint Joe around noon today. That means they had time to get back to Saint Joe after dropping it off. This probably means the trailer is still close, maybe even in Saint Joe.

"To find it, we need to talk to either the Monkeys or the guys in the blue Chevy. Both were in St. Joe today. That's where we need to start looking for them.

"What I can't figure out is why the Chevy guys wanted the trailer in the first place. Why would they take it?"

Devin had the answer. "It's a pretty new Airstream. They're easy to sell for a quick buck. Mine would bring twenty thousand on eBay or Craigslist. Even wholesale it would bring fifteen."

I nodded. Sounded like a good reason to steal one to me. "Okay, let's assume they took it to resell. What would they have to do before they could list it?"

Again, Devin had the answer. "They'd want to strip out all the personal stuff from inside. Anything that could identify the original owner. Photos, clothes, paperwork, everything except the furniture would need to be removed and destroyed. Then they'd want to grind off the serial number and create a new title or bill of sale.

"Even then they wouldn't want to list it locally. Too big a chance of getting caught. But if they had a partner up north, they could haul it up there where no one would be looking for it and sell it there. That's what I'd do."

Another good answer from Devin. So good that it made me wonder if she'd done this herself or knew people who had. I wanted to ask her about it but now was not the time. Instead, I said, "Let's say they took the trailer back to Saint Joe. What's the best way to get it there without too many people seeing it? And once there, where would be a good place to stash it?"

Devin thought for a minute. "If they had any sense, they wouldn't take 98 back to St. Joe. That's the road everyone takes. A lot of people would see it on that road. A better way would be to take 20 then get on 71. It's the back way. It takes longer and the road's not as good. But almost no one uses it.

"If you went that way, there are some places right outside St. Joe where you could hide a trailer. Abandoned barns left over from the oyster heydays. Most of them have drive-through doors for loading big trucks. It'd be real easy to hide a trailer in one of them. We should definitely check them out."

I nodded. "Yeah, probably. But here's what I think we

should do first. If we leave now, we can get back to St. Joe before dark. We can set up at an RV park there and use your Bronco to get around town. It does run, right?"

"Of course it runs. You think I'd live way out here without having decent transportation? That Bronco might look old, but it runs good. It'll outrun this motorhome, that's for sure."

"Okay, it's settled. Your Bronco can outrun the motorhome. I'll keep that in mind if I'm ever tempted to race you.

"Now, back to the plan. Kat and I will head to St. Joe in the motorhome. You follow us in the Bronco. On the way, Kat will call around and find us an RV park for the night. If we get separated, she'll call and tell you where we're going.

"Any questions?"

Devin didn't have any. She seemed anxious to get on the road. To head back to St. Joe. To find the people who took her trailer.

I didn't blame her but wanted her to be careful. "Promise me you won't go off looking for your trailer without us. And if you see the guys in the blue Chevy, you'll leave them alone. Will you promise me that?"

Devin nodded. "Sure, whatever you want."

She grabbed her duffel bag and left. I watched as she walked over to her Bronco and unlocked it. She tossed the duffel into the back seat and got in on the driver's side. I heard the whir of a starter motor followed by a low rumble coming from the Bronco's dual exhaust.

She revved the engine then rolled down her window and waved, giving us the signal to go ahead. She was ready to follow us back to St. Joe. At least that had been the plan. As it turned out, Devin wasn't much of a follower.

As soon as we pulled out of Dreamland, she goosed the Bronco and passed us in a cloud of dust. She waved as she went by and was soon out of sight. She wasn't going to wait for us or anyone else.

The motorhome needed gas so we stopped on the way out of town to fill up. While I was outside pumping, Kat stayed inside and programmed the GPS to put us on the roads she figured Devin would be taking. We would avoid US 98 and most of the traffic around Destin and Panama City. By taking the same route Devin was on, we'd be able to come to her aid if the Bronco let her down.

It turned out to be an easy trip. Not much traffic and no sign of Devin. Along the way, Kat had pulled up a list of RV parks in St. Joe and was able to book a site at a place called Indian Pass. When she told them we'd be arriving late, they said, "No problem." They'd leave the gate open for us.

Chapter Thirty-two

We'd been on the road pretty much nonstop since leaving the Ho Hum RV Park that morning. We'd traveled to Apalachicola, St. Joe, Panama City, Destin and then on to Niceville. After a few minutes in Niceville, we got back in the motorhome and drove back to St. Joe.

We'd gone a little under four hundred miles since the start of the day. It wouldn't have been a lot if we'd been on the interstate. But we weren't. We were on back roads, traveling through small towns and through the stop and go traffic around Panama City and Destin.

We'd actually only stopped a couple of times. Once for lunch at the barbeque place in St. Joe. That hadn't worked out too well for me. Instead of eating, I spent my time fighting. After lunch, we were back on the road until we got caught up in a tropical storm near Mexico Beach and had to pull over and wait it out.

When the storm passed, we continued on for a little over a hundred miles to Niceville. Then, after a few minutes there, we turned around and went back a hundred and fifty miles to St. Joe.

It was just after dark when we pulled into the Indian Pass Campground. The lights in the office were still on so I went in to settle up.

They'd given us site C-9 on the waterfront. One of their best according to the woman who checked us in. She asked me if we had any pets or children and seemed pleased when I said we didn't. Just three adults. Me, Kat and Devin. We did have a second vehicle, a white Ford Bronco, and I let her know we'd be coming and going in that.

After I paid the camping fee, I went back to the motorhome and gave Kat the map showing how to get to our site. She was happy to see it was on the water. "Should be peaceful."

I was hoping she was right. Peaceful would be a good way to spend the rest of this trip.

I backed into the site and we set up camp. While I was outside getting us hooked up, Kat called Devin and told her where we were. When I got back in, she said, "Devin's on her way. She drove by the house the Monkeys used to live in but it was gone. Said it looked like the hurricane got it. Nothing there but a vacant lot."

It didn't surprise me that even though I'd asked her not to go off on her own looking for the Monkeys, she went ahead and did it anyway. The trailer they took was her home, and if it'd been mine, I probably would have done the same thing. I would have gone out looking for the people who took it. They would have paid a price if I had found them.

"What else did she say?"

"She said we need to find her trailer tonight before whoever took it has time to empty it out or take it out of state. She thinks our best chance is to find the Trailer Monkeys. They'll either know where it is or who has it."

Devin was probably right. If we didn't find the trailer soon, it might be gone forever. If the trailer were gone, the package we were supposed to pick up for Kat's father would be gone as well. He wouldn't be happy about that. I wouldn't want to be the one who had to tell him.

The best way to avoid his wrath was to find the trailer and retrieve the package. Devin was right; we needed to start looking for it right away. While we waited for her to show up, I asked Kat about dinner. "You know this town. Where should we eat?"

She laughed. "Not the barbeque place. The food's good but the entertainment's a little rough."

I agreed with her on that. I wanted to avoid going places where I might have to fight my way out.

I was in the back of the motorhome checking on Bob when I heard the crunch of tires on the crushed oyster shell road that led to our site. Looking out the window, I saw Devin pulling up in her white Bronco. She stepped out holding a white paper bag and headed for our door.

Kat was waiting for her. "What's in the bag?"

"Tacos. I thought we should eat something before we go out bar hopping. Hope you're hungry."

I *was* hungry and glad she brought food, but I wasn't too keen on going out to the bars. "Bar hopping? You sure that's what we should be doing tonight? I thought you wanted to find the Trailer Monkeys."

"I do want to find them. The best places to look are going to be the bars in Apalachicola. Any place where they serve whiskey. That's where they hang out. At least that's where they did back in the day."

She knew them better than I did, so I couldn't argue. If we needed to look in bars, that's where we'd look. But first we needed to eat.

We sat at the kitchen table and started working on the tacos. Kat had pulled soft drinks from the fridge and we sat and ate, mostly in silence.

I still wasn't keen on hitting the bars, but if that's what it took to find the guys who hauled away her trailer, that's what we were going to do. Devin shared her plan. "Since it looks like the guys in the Monte Carlo have some kind of beef with Pico, he'll probably want to avoid them. That means he and Squally would be smart to stay out of the bars in St. Joe. They'll go to Apalach instead. They've got plenty of drinking buddies over there.

"I don't figure they'll be driving their truck with the monkey logo on the side. That'd make it too easy for the bad guys to find them. They'll be driving something else, but I don't know what. That means the only way we're going to find them is to go inside the bars and look for them."

Devin had more to say but stopped to take a bite from the taco she was holding. After washing it down with a swallow of Mountain Dew, she continued. "Pico and Squally will recognize Kat if they see her. But they probably won't remember me, and Pico may not recognize Walker. He only saw him for a few seconds today. Since we don't want to spook them, Walker and I will go in first."

She turned to Kat. "You'll have to wait outside in the Bronco."

Kat didn't like that part of the plan. "Why should I have to stay outside? Yeah, Pico and Squally will probably recognize me, but why wouldn't that be a good thing, a friendly face and all?"

Devin thought about it then said, "Okay, you can go in with us, but we need to stick together. We don't want to get separated."

She looked at me. "Walker, we don't need you starting any fights. If it looks like a fight is about to break out, just walk away. Don't be a hero."

I smiled. "Agreed. No fighting for me tonight."

We finished up our tacos, cleaned off the table and headed out. Devin was driving because we were in her Bronco and she knew the bars we needed to visit. Apalachicola was twenty-four miles east and we headed in that direction.

I was in the back seat, Devin's duffel bag beside me. I knew it had her fake pregnant belly in it. No telling what else.

Before the night was over, I'd find out.

Chapter Thirty-three

When we got to Apalach, Devin drove to Water Street where the oyster and shrimp boats dock overnight. In the old days, warehouses lined the street across from the docks and that's where they processed the daily catch and prepared it for shipping to grocers and restaurants throughout the south.

These days, only a few of the warehouses were still used for processing. Most had been converted to restaurants and bars to serve the tourist trade.

Devin parked in front of Boss Oyster, one of the nicer places on the street, and said, "We'll start here. Kat and I will go in first. You wait out here for three minutes and then you come in. Go straight to the bar and stay away from us. We don't want it to look like we're all together."

I wasn't sure why she didn't want it to look like I was with them, but I wasn't going to argue. They knew the lay of the land and I didn't.

I watched as the two girls headed inside. I waited two minutes then started to go in after them. They met me at the door, coming back out. Devin said, "They're not in there. We need to keep looking."

We tried four other bars on Water Street. Each time the girls would go in first and I'd wait outside. If they didn't come back out within five minutes, I'd go inside looking for them.

Every time I went in, both girls would have a drink in hand, always bought by men seeking their attention. The girls would thank the men and ask if they'd seen the Trailer Monkeys. Almost everyone knew who they were, but so far no one had reported seeing them that night.

After checking the bars on Water Street and coming up empty, we stopped at Honey Hole Liquors at the corner of Water and Avenue F. The people inside said they knew who the Trailer Monkeys were but added they weren't really the kind of clientele that visited their shop.

From there we headed up to Avenue D and tried the bars and restaurants on that street. Like before, it seemed no one had seen or would admit to seeing the Trailer Monkeys.

I could tell Devin was getting discouraged but she didn't give up. She said, "There's another place I want to check. It's not real nice but the drinks are cheap and I used to know the bartender there."

By my count, she and Kat had been served free drinks at five of the bars we'd visited. They'd been careful not to drink too much but even small sips from five drinks could have a cumulative effect. Devin tossed me the keys to the Bronco and said, "You drive. Go two blocks north then pull into the Piggly Wiggly parking lot."

Having grown up in the south, I knew that Piggly Wiggly was a grocery store chain and after hours the parking lots were often a meeting place for local teens.

The Piggly Wiggly in Apalach was no different. The store had closed hours earlier but there were still plenty of cars in the lot. When I pulled in, Devin pointed and said, "Over there. Park under the light."

There weren't any other cars under the light, the local youths apparently preferring the shadows. I pulled the

Bronco next to the light pole and parked. I turned to Devin as she seemed to be running the show. "Now what?"

She pointed to a run-down two story building across the street. An open door on the bottom floor led to a narrow stairway going up. "There's a bar up there. Kat and I'll go in first. You follow a few minutes later. Sit by the bar but not near us. Then just play along."

She opened the passenger door and carefully stepped out. She wasn't drunk but probably couldn't pass a sobriety test. Kat wasn't much better. They held on to each other as they crossed the street, probably hamming it up for my benefit.

When they reached the open door at the stairway, they stood up straight, adjusted their clothes and headed up.

The windows on the second floor were blacked out and I couldn't see in. If something happened to the girls up there, there was no way I would know about it until either the police or EMTs showed up.

This reminded me of waiting for them in the Walmart parking lot back in Perry. That hadn't gone well. Kat's father had made it clear I shouldn't have waited outside even though they'd told me to. I should have gone in with them.

If something happened to her tonight while I was again waiting outside, her father wouldn't be nearly so understanding. He would take it out of my hide. Not wanting to face that prospect, I locked the doors and headed across to the street to join the girls on the second floor.

Going up the stairs, I could see a closed door at the top. From the other side, I could hear people talking and laughing over a background of Delta blues. It sounded like everyone was having a good time.

I opened the door and was surprised at what I saw. From the outside, it looked like just another derelict building in a bad neighborhood, but inside the place had the vibe of a high class piano bar in an upscale neighborhood.

Looking around, I saw Kat and Devin seated at the bar having a conversation with one of the bartenders. An attractive blonde in a tight fitting top.

Remembering what Devin had told me about not sitting close to them, I walked to the far end of the bar and took a seat. The blonde looked up at me and I nodded. The universal signal for a drink. She smiled and whispered something to Devin that made her laugh. Then she grabbed a shot glass, poured a drink and brought it over to me.

"Compliments of the two girls."

She nodded at Devin and Kat and then walked back to continue her conversation. While they were talking, I took a sip of my drink expecting hard liquor. It wasn't. It was Coke, straight up. No whiskey or rum mixed in, just Coke. The girls were making sure that at least one of us stayed sober.

As I drank my Coke, I watched the bartender scribble something on a napkin and hand it to Kat. Then she looked in my direction and winked.

Kat and Devin stood and walked to the door. Devin looked over her shoulder and mouthed, "Follow us." I didn't know whether she wanted me to wait a few minutes or follow immediately. I finished off the Coke and headed for the door. As I passed the bartender, she said, "Hope to see you soon."

I wasn't sure what she meant by that. Maybe she said it to everyone as they left. Just her way of being nice.

Downstairs, the girls were waiting for me at the door. Devin spoke first. "The bartender knows where they live. It's not in St. Joe. It's here in Apalachicola. Not too far from here. She said not to go at night. Too dangerous. She said the

174

best time to find them was early morning."

I nodded. "OK, so we're going out there tonight, right?"

I figured Devin wouldn't want to wait. Even though it might be dangerous, she'd want to go out there tonight.

"Yeah, let's go out there and take a look. But first I'm supposed to give you this."

She handed me the napkin the bartender had given her. Written on it was, "I'm off tomorrow night. Give me a call. Brandi."

Devin smiled. "So are you going to call her? She really, really wants to meet you. We promised her you'd call. You're not going to disappoint her, are you?"

I decided to play along. "Sure, I'll call her. Maybe we'll hit it off. You don't mind if I borrow your Bronco to take her out, do you?"

Before she could answer, we heard glass breaking in the Piggly Wiggly parking lot. It sounded close to where we'd parked the Bronco.

Chapter Thirty-four

"You girls stay here. I'm going to go check it out."

I walked across the street and saw three men standing next to the same blue Monte Carlo we'd seen in the barbeque lot earlier in the day. They had an open twelve pack of beer on the hood of their car with just four beers left.

They were watching a group of girls on the other side of the lot and hadn't seen me. I planned to keep it that way. I didn't need any trouble with them tonight. I still had the keys to Bronco, but in order to get to it, I'd have to step out of the shadows and walk under the bright light where we'd parked.

The three men were laughing and joking and weren't paying attention to the Bronco. They wouldn't have any reason to think that the guy driving it was the same guy who interfered with their fight with Pico earlier in the day.

They were probably just drinking and blowing off steam. At least, that was my hope. I waited until all three were facing away from me and used that opportunity to walk to the driver's side door. I put the key in the lock, unlocked the door and was almost inside when someone grabbed me from behind. As they pulled me out, I tossed the keys onto the driver's seat.

One of the men had recognized me and had raced across the parking lot to get me. He called out to the others and they came running. The one who'd gotten me from behind had me in a neck hold, the same kind used to hold Pico earlier in the day. He had my arms behind my head, leaving my face and the front of my body exposed to the other two men.

They didn't wait long to start punching.

The first blow hurt the most. A straight punch to my stomach. It was quickly followed by two more. It left me gasping for air. The next was an open hand slap to the left side of my face. The man who'd hit me was wearing a ring and I felt it cut into my skin just below my eye. He followed up with two more open hand slaps. By the third one, my vision was blurred and my ears were ringing.

I lost count after that. Maybe five, maybe ten punches to my stomach and ribs before they stopped. One of the men spoke up. "So, you're Pico's friend. You want to tell me where he's hiding? Or you need some more softening up?"

I didn't need any more softening. They'd done a good job of it. But I couldn't tell them what they wanted to know. I didn't know where Pico was. I didn't figure they'd believe me if I told them that. I was trying to come up with a good answer when the man holding me from behind screamed and dropped to the ground, releasing me on the way down.

The eyes of the two men who'd been punching me lit up with fear. Something behind me had scared them. I turned and saw Devin, all five foot two of her, holding a three foot long cattle prod. Electricity crackled between the two silver electrodes at the end. She looked at me and asked, "You know how to use this?"

I nodded and she handed it to me then got into the Bronco with Kat and locked the doors. They were going to sit in safety and watch the show.

With one man down on the ground there were two left

to deal with. Both had moved a step backwards when Devin had handed me the cattle prod, but they were still within striking distance and I had a few punches I needed to repay.

With the prod pointed in his direction, I made a move toward the taller of the two men. He was big but slow. I tapped his belly with the tip of the prod sending an electric charge through his body. His eyes bulged, his head snapped back and he dropped to the ground.

The third man didn't wait around for his turn. He ran back to the Monte Carlo and jumped inside, locking the doors just like the girls had done in the Bronco.

His two buddies were still on the ground and my head and body still hurt from their beating. I was tempted to give them another taste of the prod's medicine but thought better of it. I wanted to hurt them, not kill them.

Kat rolled down her window. "Get in, we need to go."

I slid into the back seat, next to the now open duffel bag. Kat peeled out of the parking lot and hung a right. She made a left and then a right and kept going straight until we reached 98. When traffic cleared, she turned right and headed toward St. Joe.

About a mile past the airport, she slowed the Bronco and turned onto county road 385. It was narrow, unpaved, and full of potholes. No streetlights and no houses. Just a narrow strip of dirt heading away from the main road. After she'd gone about mile, she coasted to a stop.

Devin got out of the passenger seat and climbed in the back with me. Her duffel bag sat between us. She had a small flashlight in her hand and shone it in my face. "You look terrible. Does it hurt?"

It was a stupid question. "Yeah, it hurts."

She smiled. "Let me fix you up. But first hand over the

prod."

It was still in my hand. I'd been holding it ever since we left the parking lot like it was some kind of magic wand that could scare away attackers. I no longer needed it so I handed it to her. She dropped it into her duffel and pulled out a first aid kit. She put the duffel behind the seat and slid over close to me.

"This might hurt a bit." She had an alcohol swab in her right hand, moving it toward my face. I stopped her. "You sure you know what you're doing?"

"Yeah, I've fixed up a lot of guys after fights. Just hold still and I'll take care of you."

She swabbed the cut under my eye with alcohol then pulled out a tube of antibiotic ointment. She squeezed a dab of ointment onto her finger and gently spread it over the open cut on my face. When she moved in to inspect her work, I could feel the heat of her breath on my skin. We locked eyes and, for a brief moment, I felt a stirring inside. It didn't last long.

She moved back, tapped my ribs and asked, "Does that hurt?"

"Yeah, that hurts."

"Good. Take a deep breath and hold it."

It sounded like she knew what she was doing so I did what she said. I took a breath and felt a burning pain in my ribs as my chest expanded with incoming air. I held it until she said, "Okay, breathe normally."

She leaned over and put her ear on my chest and when she did, I rested my chin on her head. "Breathe," she said. "Slowly. In and out until I tell you to stop."

Again, I complied. This time the pain wasn't so bad.

180

I kept breathing, my head resting on hers. It felt good.

Finally, she leaned back and said, "Ribs aren't broken. You're going to be sore for a few days. No dancing or wrestling anytime soon but you'll be able to drive tomorrow."

She flicked off her flashlight, patted my shoulder and spoke to Kat. "We going down there or what?"

Chapter Thirty-five

Kat was in the driver's seat. Devin was in the back next to me. We were parked with our headlights off on a dirt road about three miles outside Apalachicola. Devin had just tended to the wounds I'd received at the hands of the three guys in the Monte Carlo, the same three we'd seen putting a beating on Pico earlier in the day. A beating interrupted by me.

Now it was almost midnight and we were trying to find Pico and his brother because they might know where we could find Devin's trailer.

Kat answered Devin's question. "The bartender said it was dangerous to come out here at night. She said we'd have better luck finding them in the morning. But it's your call. We'll do whatever you want."

Devin turned to me. "You feeling okay?"

I wasn't. I was in pain. But not so much that I needed to bail out on the girls. "I'm good. Whatever you want to do, count me in."

She turned to Kat. "You heard him. Let's go see if they're home."

Kat started the Bronco, turned on the headlights and we headed down the narrow road. She did her best to dodge the largest of the potholes but the rough riding Bronco shook with each one we hit.

"Tell me again why we're going down this road."

Devin was quick with the answer. "Brandi, the bartender, the one back there that wants to meet you, she said Pico and Squally were living in a stilt house at the end of Dry Bones Road. It's off this road. She said Dry Bones is not a county road and it's not maintained. According to her, it's not much more than a cow path that turns off of the road we're on.

"She said when it rains like it did today, there's a spot in the road that gets pretty muddy and it's easy to get stuck. She said if we drive into that hole and get stuck there won't be anyone around to pull us out."

Kat hit the brakes and brought the Bronco to a sudden stop. "Looks like this is the spot she was warning us about."

Outside, just ahead of us, the headlights shone on a mud hole that stretched across the full width of the road. A set of tracks sunk deep in the hole suggested it could be a problem getting through.

"What do you think? Should we try to cross it?"

I knew we were in a Bronco but didn't know whether it was four wheel drive or not. I hadn't bothered to look. With four wheel drive we could probably get through the mud; without it maybe not. I decided to ask. "Is this four wheel drive?"

It was Devin's Bronco. She was still sitting in the back beside me. "No. It's not."

I didn't say anything but I remembered the many times back on the farm when I'd had gotten our truck stuck in the mud and either had to get someone to pull me out or ended up spending the night in the truck waiting for help to arrive. With the pain in my ribs, I wasn't looking forward to doing either tonight.

Devin climbed out of the Bronco and walked to the edge of the mud hole. She picked up a stick from the side of the road and pushed it into the mud. It went down a foot without any resistance. She kept pushing until the stick disappeared.

She shook her head and walked back to the driver's side. Kat rolled down the window and Devin leaned in. "It's pretty deep near the edge. Probably deeper in the middle. Not sure we could make it through without getting stuck. I don't think we should try."

She opened the driver's door. "My turn to drive."

It was Devin's Bronco and she knew how to drive it better than Kat. They traded seats. I stayed in the back and held on.

Devin put the Bronco in reverse and backed up until she found a spot in the road wide enough to turn it around. It took her three tries to get it going in the right direction, but she finally did.

She kept going until we reached US 98. She wasn't really happy about having to go back to the motorhome without finding her trailer, but there was no sense in getting stuck in a mud hole and having to sleep in the Bronco.

It was a relief when we pulled up in front of our campsite at Indian Pass. Bob met us at the door of the motorhome, happy we were back. Unlike the previous evening, there were no discussions about sleeping arrangements. We were all too tired to change things around. Kat slept in the back bedroom with me. Devin and Bob slept up front on the couch. The pain in my ribs kept me awake until I got up and took a couple of Advil. After that, I slept a baby.

Or at least I thought I did.

Chapter Thirty-six

"Walker, you kept me awake most of the night. Snoring and grunting like a wild hog rooting around in the woods. I was afraid the people next door would come over and complain."

Kat was sitting at the kitchen table, dark circles under her eyes, a can of Mountain Dew in her hand. "And why don't you have any coffee in this place? What kind of heathen are you?"

I raised my hands in surrender. "Kat, I'm sorry about the snoring. Next time three guys jump me, I'll ask them not to hit me in the face 'cause it makes me snore and it keeps you awake at night.

"Now, about the coffee, that Mountain Dew you're drinking has lot more caffeine than coffee and it's easier to make. Just pop the top and you're in business."

Devin was on the couch listening and I could hear her laugh. "You two sound like an old married couple. Complaining about everything."

She looked at Kat. "Your problem is you had too many rum and cokes last night. You have a hangover and you're taking it out on Walker.

"Poor guy got beat up defending our honor. If I hadn't come to his rescue with the cattle prod, he'd probably be in the hospital or maybe even the morgue. So give him a break."

Kat finished off her Mountain Dew in one long swallow.

She stood, burped loudly and said, "I'll be in the bathroom. I expect both of you to be ready to go when I come out."

Devin looked like she'd already gotten ready. Her hair was combed, her clothes looked fresh; she looked more than ready for whatever adventures lay ahead.

I, on the other hand, hurt. My head, my face, my ribs, and my belly. With each breath, the pain in my ribs reminded me of the punches I'd taken the night before. It hadn't been the worst beating I'd gotten, not by a long shot, but it still hurt. I was hoping a little ibuprofen would take care of it. I grabbed a Mountain Dew from the fridge, popped two Advil and washed them down.

I was wearing the same clothes I'd worn the day before. I planned to wear them again. No need to change if we were going back out on Dry Bones Road looking for Pico and Squally. Chances were good I'd be the one having to dig the Bronco out of the mud.

When Kat came out the bathroom, she pointed back over her shoulder. "Bob left you a big present in the litter box. You might want to clean it up before we leave. I'm sure he'd appreciate it."

She walked past me and as she did, she nudged me in the ribs. It hurt, but I wasn't going to let her know. Instead, I reached up into the cabinet near the sink, pulled out an empty Publix grocery bag and headed to the bathroom to empty the litter box.

Kat's description of what Bob had left me was an understatement. The two girls staying with us in the motorhome clearly had not interfered with his bowel movements. They appeared to be on schedule and plenty robust. His box was fuller than he liked and I knew from experience he wouldn't be happy with the situation. He'd soon be looking for an alternate location to relieve himself.

Several months earlier, when I'd neglected to clean his box, he'd left me a reminder. In the middle of the night, he made a deposit in my shoe. A large one. He was sending me a message. One that was sure to get my attention.

Since the shoe incident, I've been pretty good about keeping his box clean. And Bob's been pretty good about using it instead of my footwear.

I cleaned out his box, put the clumps in the plastic bag and tied it off. I made sure his food and water bowls were full then washed my hands and face. It was the first time I'd looked in the mirror since the fight. I had a cut on my left cheek and darkening bruises around both eyes. They would soon turn purple. I looked like a prize fighter—the one who'd lost the fight.

I left the bathroom carrying the plastic bag full of Bob's gifts. He was sitting on the couch between Kat and Devin, purring loudly. I was pretty sure he was happy to see me carrying the litter filled bag. It meant a lot to him whenever I took care of his business.

Devin stood. "If we leave now, we'll have time to stop at McDonald's and get breakfast. But we need to hurry if we plan to find Pico."

The clock over the kitchen sink showed six forty-five. Plenty early for me. But according to Devin, Brandi had said if we wanted to find Pico and Squally, we needed to go out to their place early. Before ten.

If we left now, we should make it in plenty of time.

Outside, I dropped Bob's litter into the trash barrel and hopped in the back of the Bronco. Devin had slid into the driver's seat and Kat had called shotgun.

We left the campground with Devin at the wheel. She

knew her way around, so she was driving. The first stop was the McDonald's drive-through on US 98. We all ordered the same thing—sausage and egg biscuits. Easy to eat on the road. Kat ordered a coffee.

There was an Advance Auto Parts store across the street and it looked like they were getting ready to open. I pointed to it and asked Devin to pull in.

"Why do we need to go there?"

"To get a tow strap. You don't have one, do you?"

"No. You think we'll need one?"

"We might. If we get stuck in the mud, a tow strap might come in handy. Be better to have it and not need it than to need it and not have one."

Devin pointed over her shoulder. "I've got a winch, a portable one that hooks to the bumper. It's in the back in that black bag."

I looked over my shoulder to see what was in the back. A spare tire, a portable air compressor, a baseball bat and a bag with the word 'Super Winch' stenciled in white on the outside.

"Does it work?"

She shrugged. "Don't know. Never tried it. Don't even know how to hook it up. But the guy who sold me the Bronco said it worked."

I nodded. "Good, maybe we'll find out if it does. But just in case it doesn't, pull in the parts store, let me pick up a tow strap."

Devin relented and pulled into the parking spot closest to the door. She and Kat stayed in the Bronco and ate their breakfast biscuits while I ran in and bought a tow strap. Bright yellow with forged steel hooks on either end, rated to tow ten thousand pounds. I put it on my credit card and headed back outside.

I threw the strap in the back next to the winch and we got back on the road. Devin headed east on 98, toward Apalachicola. Twenty minutes later, we were back on county road 385. Overnight, the road hadn't magically improved. It was still bumpy, still narrow, and still mostly dirt with an uneven layer of crushed oyster shells on top. The only good thing about it was, in the daylight, Devin could see the bigger potholes and steer around them.

Many of the potholes were unavoidable and I could feel each one she hit in my ribs. Each one she missed was a blessing. Unfortunately, the further we went down the road, the bigger and more frequent the potholes were. Most were filled with water left over from the previous day's rain. Devin had to drive slowly to keep from shaking the Bronco to pieces.

It took us twenty minutes to reach the mud hole that had stopped us the night before. She pulled up to the edge of it and asked, "What do you think?"

Instead of answering, I popped open my door and got out to take a closer look. The mud hole stretched the full width of the road. The fences lining both sides meant there was no way around it. If we wanted to keep going, we'd have to get through.

I picked up a rock and tossed it into the middle of the hole. It made a 'kerplunk' sound and disappeared into the muck. That didn't tell me much about how deep the hole was, other than it was at least deep enough to cover the rock.

There were really only two ways to find out how deep it really was. Either walk out into it and see how far I sank or get Devin to drive the Bronco through. My vote was for trying it in the Bronco.

While thinking about what we'd have to do if we got stuck, the size and location of the mud hole made me wonder. The other potholes on the road were small, most not much bigger than a basketball. And most had sand in the bottom, not mud.

This one was different. Instead of being round like the others, this was almost a perfect rectangle. It stretched the full width of the road and was three car lengths long.

It was as if someone intentionally created this hole as a way to discourage people from traveling further down the road. I'd seen this before. Back in Arkansas. People growing pot out in the woods would create these kinds of obstacles to keep prying eyes from finding their stash.

The more I thought about it the more this one looked intentional. You didn't get mud like this on these kinds of roads in Florida. Someone had made this to keep people out. People like us.

I walked back to the Bronco and got in. Devin was waiting to hear what I thought. "So?"

I shrugged. "It's mud. It's deep. And we'll probably get stuck. But if Pico and Squally live down this road and you want to go see them, we've got to go through it.

"Here's what I suggest. Back up about fifty feet, enough room to get a running start. Then floor it and hit the hole at full speed. Keep the wheels straight and hold on until we get to the other side. If we're lucky, the momentum will carry us across."

Devin nodded, put it in reverse and backed the Bronco up a good hundred feet. She put it in drive, gunned the motor and said, "Hold On!"

Chapter Thirty-seven

We were doing a little over forty when we hit the mud. The speed helped the heavy Bronco cover more than half the distance across the hole before it began to sink in. Devin kept the power up as the Bronco struggled to climb out, but the slick mud caused the tires to lose their grip.

We could hear the roar of the engine and the whine of the spinning tires but we weren't making much headway. The Bronco didn't give up though. It kept trying to pull us through, even as it settled further down into the mud.

The settling is what saved us. The heavy Bronco continued to sink until its rear tires reached the solid ground below the mud. Gaining instant traction, it jumped the last few yards out of the hole, putting us on solid ground on the other side.

Devin immediately got off the gas and let the Bronco coast to a stop. She killed the engine, opened her door and stepped out.

"Look at all the mud on my poor truck!"

Kat and I got out to take a look. A thick layer of mud coated the outside of the Bronco. It had been white before we hit the hole; now it was mostly brown from the top down.

Behind the truck, the mud hole had two deep ruts left by the spinning tires. Judging by how fast the ruts were filling in with water, it was unlikely anyone in anything other than a high centered truck or SUV would be making it through that day.

Devin looked admiringly at her Bronco. "My baby got us through. I'll have to treat her to a bath later on."

She got back in on the driver's side and started the motor. Not wanting to be left behind, Kat and I joined her inside. According to what Brandi had said, Dry Bones Road would be off to our right. She had warned it would be easy to miss. It wasn't much more than a grass covered track.

Devin drove slowly, avoiding potholes while looking for our turn. After three miles, she found it. It was exactly as the bartender had described; a single track through the grass.

She made the turn and continued on until the road ended in an open field in front of a stilt house. Like many houses in this area, this one was built on poles, elevated fifteen feet above the ground. Designed so flood waters wouldn't wash it away. A stairway from the ground led up to a deck that wrapped all the way around the outside.

Anyone living here would have a great view of the surrounding area. With no nearby neighbors, they'd have the privacy to do whatever they wanted—including getting rid of unwanted visitors like us.

Devin spoke first. "There aren't any cars here. No lights on inside. Doesn't look like anyone is home."

I opened my door and stepped out into the low grass. I waited to see if a dog would come running. Most people who live this far out have dogs. Big ones. They make excellent early warning systems and keep would-be trespassers from getting out of their vehicles.

I whistled, loud enough to wake a sleeping dog, and waited. Not hearing a bark, I shouted, "Hey, anyone home?"

Again, I waited.

There was no response. Not from dogs. Not from people.

Devin and Kat were still inside the Bronco letting me be the dog bait. When they saw there were no dogs chasing me or people coming out with guns, they joined me in the yard.

I pointed at the house. "It doesn't look like anyone lives there. There's none of the things you'd expect to see. No cars, no trash, no pets. Not even a lawn mower."

Devin nodded. "You're right. It looks vacant. You think Brandi sent us on a wild goose chase?"

I shrugged. "I don't know; you talked to her. But since we're here, I'm going to go check it out."

I was pretty sure there weren't any dogs on the property. But, playing it safe, I stopped after every few steps and listened. My plan was simple. If I heard or saw a dog running in my direction, especially a big one, I was going to head back to the Bronco as fast as I could. If I couldn't get inside, I'd get on top.

I probably couldn't outrun a dog, but I'd sure try.

Fortunately, I didn't have to find out. I made it all the way to the house without seeing or hearing one.

With most stilt houses, you expect to find things like lawn mowers, boats and outdoor furniture stored underneath, out of the weather. There was nothing under this one. Just a paved area with a few oil spots. They looked like they'd been there a long time.

I made my way over to the stairs and again let my presence be known. "Hey, anyone up there?"

I listened for a response, including movement in the house, but heard nothing. If anyone was home, they were either passed out or dead. I was hoping it was neither.

I made my way up the stairs, checking over my shoulder

to make sure the girls were still waiting for me at the Bronco. And also to make sure nothing was following me up.

At the top, I stepped to the door, opened the screen and knocked. Again, I listened, trying to hear movement from inside. And, as before, nothing.

I was pretty confident no one was home. Still, I wanted to be absolutely sure. I closed the screen door and walked to the large picture window beside it. The window would have given anyone inside a clear view of cars pulling into the yard. It would also give anyone standing on the deck a clear view into the house—if the curtains were open. Today they weren't. They were closed.

I walked around the deck checking each window, hoping the curtains were open so I could see inside. They were closed on all the windows facing the yard. They were also closed on the north side of the house.

But on the east side, I got lucky. No curtains on the first window I checked. Looking in, I could see what was probably a laundry room. There were washer and dryer hookups, but no washer or dryer. There were no curtains on the next three windows either. One looked in on a room with two twin beds. Bare mattresses, no sheets, no pillows. An empty closet with an open door.

The next window looked in on a small bathroom. Sink, toilet and shower. Reasonably clean, but no towels or other things you'd see in a bathroom in a house where people actually lived.

I continued my walk around the deck, finally ending up back where I started, at the front door. The girls had made their way to the bottom of the stairs, just below where I was standing.

Devin looked up and asked, "Anyone inside?"

"No. Doesn't look like anyone lives here. There are no clothes or anything. Just an empty house."

She turned and looked back at the Bronco then back at me. "My Airstream's not here either. Brandi screwed us. Next time I see her, there's going to be trouble."

I remembered Devin had given me a note the night before with Brandi's number on it. She'd made a joke saying the bartender wanted me to call her about a date. Maybe that was it or maybe she wanted me to call for another reason.

I got the note out my pocket, looked at the number and decided now would be a good time to call.

Brandi answered on the third ring. "Hey, what's going on?"

"Nothing much, how about you?"

"Just chilling. Who am I talking to?"

"Walker. From the bar last night. You gave a note to Devin to give to me. Said to call you. Remember?"

"Maybe. Tell me more about the girl I gave the note to."

"There were two of them. One looks like a young Joan Jett. The other one could pass for her sister, a little taller. They asked about Pico and Squally."

That seemed to stir her memory.

"Oh yeah, I remember them."

"Good. Do you remember what you told them? About where to find Pico and Squally?"

She laughed. "Yeah, I remember. I sent them on a wild goose chase down Bones Road. Did the same with the other guys who were asking about them."

"Other guys?"

"Yeah, after the girls left, three guys came in asking me if I knew where to find Pico and Squally. I told them the same thing I told your two friends. Look down Dry Bones Road.

"They took off without ordering drinks or leaving me a tip. But that's okay, because they're not going to find Pico and Squally out there."

"Why not?"

"Because Pico and Squally don't live on Dry Bones Road. No one does. Not since the last people who lived there got busted for growing pot."

She laughed again. "You didn't go out there looking for them, did you?"

I wasn't going to tell her the truth. No need to give her the satisfaction. "No, I'm in town. Still looking for Pico though. He ordered a part for his truck and I need to get it to him."

I was hoping she'd take the bait and give me Pico's address. But she didn't.

Instead she said, "Pico's not at his place anymore. He ran into some money problems and had to move. Not sure where to. His brother probably knows. He lives in St. Joe."

"His brother? You're talking about Squally, right?"

"No, not Squally. He's the one who caused the money problems. He's worse off than Pico. I'm talking about his other brother. He'll know where to find him."

This was our first solid lead, assuming she was telling the truth. I decided to dig a little deeper.

"You tell the other guys that? To look in St. Joe for Pico?"

"No. I got the feeling they were looking for payback. Pico doesn't need that in his life. Not now. He's got enough to deal with as it is."

I wasn't sure what she meant by that and really didn't care. I just wanted to know where to find him and his brother. Mostly, I wanted to find Devin's trailer and get the package I was supposed to take back to Kat's father.

"So you say Pico might be at his brother's place in St. Joe. Where exactly is that?"

She laughed. "The only way you're going to find that out is if you take me to dinner tonight. Do me right and I just might tell you. But only after. Think about it and call me back."

She ended the call.

Chapter Thirty-eight

The girls were waiting for me in the Bronco. They were in the front so I climbed in the back. As soon as I got in, Devin asked, "Who were you talking to?"

"Your friend from the bar. The one who sent you out here."

"You mean Brandi. What'd she have to say?"

"She said Pico and Squally don't live here, never have. Said we'd probably find them at their brother's place in St. Joe. But she wouldn't give me the address."

Kat stopped me. "Pico and Squally have a brother? That's news to me. When I dated Squally, Pico was his only brother. That was eight years ago. I don't think they grew another one since then."

I shrugged. "That's what she said. They'd be hiding at his brother's place."

"What else did she tell you?"

"She said we weren't the only ones looking for Pico and Squally. Three other guys, probably the ones you zapped in the parking lot, came in looking for them. She said she sent them on the same wild goose chase she sent us on."

Devin started the Bronco. "If those guys are coming out here today, we need to leave."

She put the Bronco in gear, did a U-turn and headed back out the way we'd come in. She tapped the steering wheel and asked, "What else did she say? Any clues as to where Pico's brother lives?"

"No, only that he's in St. Joe. She did say that if I took her to dinner tonight, she'd tell me more. Then she hung up."

Kat turned around and looked at me. In an angry voice, she asked, "Did you call to ask her out on a date? I hope not because we're supposed to be looking for Devin's trailer, not trying to find you a date for tonight."

Kat's anger caught me by surprise. I wasn't sure what was behind it but I didn't want it directed at me.

"Kat, I didn't call her to get a date. I called because I thought she might know more than she told you. Right now, she's our only lead and I have no desire to go out with her. I'd prefer never to see or talk to her again. But if we don't find the trailer today, I might have to. She might be the only way we find Pico and Squally. Unless you have a better idea."

Kat turned to Devin. "Can you believe it? He's still talking about seeing her. Maybe we should let him walk back from here. That'll give him plenty of time to think about his night ahead with Brandi."

I wasn't sure whether she was kidding or not but I didn't want to walk back, so I decided to give her a reason not to leave me behind. "How about this? We go back to the motorhome; I'll get out my computer and see if I can find anything that links Pico or Squally to an address in St. Joe.

"I can do a property search, see if anything shows up. I can search court records, driver's license databases, voter registration. Whatever it takes. It won't take long and we might get lucky. But if you put me out here and make me walk back, it's not going to happen."

Kat shook her head and looked at Devin. She didn't say anything and Devin didn't either. I was waiting to see what her answer would be when the Bronco suddenly slowed.

From the front seat, Devin said, "Looks like we have company."

Up ahead, the blue Monte Carlo sat in the middle of the mud hole. Three men were sitting on its hood, covered in mud. At first, they looked happy to see us, hoping for a rescue. When they realized who we were, their happiness faded.

Devin let the Bronco roll to a stop. "What should we do?"

Kat answered, "We can't do anything. They're blocking the road. We can't get past them and they can't get past us."

I had an idea. "Let me go talk to them."

I stepped out, held my arms palms up so they could see I was unarmed and walked in their direction. One of the men, the smallest of the three, said something to the others then slid off the car hood and took three muddy steps in my direction. He was coming out to meet me. It didn't look like he was armed.

On his fourth step, his boot sunk in the mud. When he tried to take another step, his foot came out of the boot and he almost fell forward. He regained his balance and put his bare foot back into the mud stuck boot. He wasn't going anywhere soon.

I took the opportunity to speak. "Looks like you're stuck."

He nodded. "Yeah, we are. So are you."

I pointed back at the Bronco. "We have a tow strap. Might be able to pull you out, but we should probably talk first."

"Talk? You mean you don't want to fight?"

I hoped he was making a joke.

"No, I don't want to fight. Not yet. Maybe it'll come to that later. But let's talk first."

"What you want to talk about?"

"The Airstream trailer. The one that was stolen from Niceville. It belongs to my friend back there."

He shook his head. "We didn't steal the trailer. We paid for it. We got a bill of sale as proof."

I nodded. "You might have a bill of sale, but whoever took your money didn't own that trailer. Devin, the girl in the Bronco behind me, she owns it."

He was still shaking his head. "No, the man who sold it to us, he said it was his. He signed the bill of sale. Let me talk to the girl."

I walked back to the Bronco and got Devin. I told her what the man said about buying her trailer. She couldn't wait to talk to him. She climbed out of the Bronco and walked to the mud hole. She looked at the man and said, "Where's my trailer?"

He shook his head. "You got it wrong. It's my trailer now. I paid good money for it. I got a bill of sale."

Devin didn't care. "No, you're the one who's got it wrong. It's my trailer. It's titled in my name. Devin McSweeney. A title search will show I own it."

"You're a McSweeney?"

Devin nodded. "Yeah."

"You related to Dan McSweeney?"

"Yeah, he's my father. David and Dale are my brothers. You know them?"

The man looked down at his feet then back up at Devin.

"You're saying you're Dan McSweeney's daughter? Any proof?"

"Yeah, I got proof. It says McSweeney on my driver's license. But maybe that's not enough for you. Why don't I call my dad right now? You can explain to him why you stole the Airstream trailer he bought for me."

The man held up both arms, palms up, just like I had done a few minutes earlier. A sign of peace or conciliation. No longer argumentative, he said, "No, don't call. There's no need to bother him. I believe you. It's your trailer and we didn't mean to take it. It's just that the man who sold it to us said he was the owner and we paid him good money for it."

Devin nodded. "So you're saying you didn't mean to steal my trailer. It was an honest mistake, right?"

"Yeah, that's what it was. An honest mistake. We thought we were buying it from the owner. He had the all the right paperwork."

Devin nodded. "Okay then. We're getting somewhere. Tell me your name."

He hesitated, probably worried that giving Devin his name might get him in trouble. She saw his hesitation and said, "Just your first name. So we can talk like civilized people."

He smiled. "They call me Dabbo. The two guys behind me are Diego and Luis. Luis is the big one."

Devin smiled. "Dabbo, tell me about the man who sold you my trailer. How did he get in touch with you?"

Dabbo looked down at his feet, still stuck in the mud. He looked up and said, "Get me out of this and I'll tell you everything. We'll even help you get your trailer back."

Devin turned to me. "Think you can pull the car out?"

I was pretty sure the Bronco could do it. It would be messy, but it could be done. "Yeah, I think we can get it out."

"Let's do it then."

I went back to the Bronco, started it and moved it closer to the mud hole. I left enough so I could get down on the ground and hook up the tow strap.

I grabbed the tow strap from the back and connected one end to the tie down hooks under the Bronco's front end. Almost all cars these days have these kinds of hooks. They're added at the factory, welded to the frame, right behind the front bumper. They're used to tie down new cars to keep them from falling off transport trucks when they're shipped to the dealer.

With one end of the tow strap secured to the Bronco, I tossed the other end to Dabbo. "Hook it under the bumper onto something strong. The tow hooks if you have them. Don't hook it to the bumper because it's just plastic and it'll pull right off."

Dabbo nodded like he understood. He was standing in the mud and it took him some effort to drag the tow strap to his car and get it hooked up. While he was busy doing that, I asked Kat and Devin to get back into the Bronco. I didn't want either of them to get hurt if the tow strap snapped or something went wrong when we started pulling the car.

When Dabbo signaled me he was ready, I told him what to do next. "Get your buddies to stand back behind the car out of the way. You get in, start it up and put it in drive. When I honk my horn, take your foot off the brakes, give it some gas and I'll start pulling. When you see me stop, you stop. Don't run into me."

I got into the Bronco and put it in reverse. I tapped the horn to signal Dabbo I was about to start pulling. Instead of stomping on the gas, I feathered it, watching the slack slowly go out of the tow strap. When the strap went taut, I gave the Bronco a little more gas.

The Bronco, being heavier and having a lot of horsepower, had no problem pulling the Monte Carlo. My only real concern was the tow strap. Even though it was rated at ten thousand pounds, the combined weight of the Bronco and Monte Carlo, along with all the mud we would be dragging, would push the strap to its limit.

If it broke, there'd be a lot of energy in the part of the strap that went flying through the air. If it still had the heavy hook at the end, it could kill anyone who got in the way. I didn't want that.

I kept my eye on the strap as we slowly pulled the car out. Dabbo kept the front wheels on the Monte Carlo heading in the right direction and gave the car enough gas to keep the back wheels spinning slowly. Too much and the spinning wheels could break an axle when they connected with solid ground. Dabbo apparently knew this and was careful with the pedal.

It took a little more than two minutes to pull the Monte Carlo to where it's front tires were on solid ground. As soon as they were, I gave Dabbo a thumbs up to let him know we were close.

A moment later, his rear tires gained traction and he was able to drive the final few feet out of the hole under his own power. When there was ten feet of space between the back of his car and the edge of the hole, I honked my horn, letting him know it was time to stop.

He hit his brakes, put his car in park and smiled. He was happy to be free of the mud. But he knew he would have to go back through it again to get to the highway.

I killed the motor on the Bronco and got out. Kat and Devin got out as well. We watched as Dabbo, who was still in his car, opened his glove compartment and rooted around for something. I turned to the girls and said, "I don't think he's looking for a gun, but it might be a good idea to stand behind the door just in case."

The girls quickly moved behind the open passenger door of the Bronco. It wasn't bullet proof but would be better than standing out in the open if someone started shooting in our direction.

Dabbo's two companions, Luis and Diego, who had watched from the back side of the mud hole, now had to make a choice. Either stay where they were or climb over the barbed wire fence on the side of the road and make their way to where we were standing.

They decided to climb the fence.

Chapter Thirty-nine

Dabbo came out of the Monte Carlo with papers in his hand. "This is the bill of sale. You can see it shows we bought an Airstream trailer from the guy who signed on the bottom. This second sheet is the shipping contract we signed with the Trailer Monkeys. They were supposed to pick up the trailer and haul it to our shop in Apalachicola."

He handed the papers to Devin. She glanced at them and then asked Dabbo, "How did this guy get in touch with you about buying the trailer?"

Dabbo didn't hesitate with his answer. "Craigslist. We run ads all over the state saying we buy Airstreams. He saw our ad and called us. Said he had one for sale."

Devin nodded. "Then what?"

"He said he bought the trailer for his girlfriend. She was living in it in Niceville. Said his girlfriend broke up with him and moved out. The trailer was empty and he wanted to sell it before his wife found out about it.

"He said it was a twenty-seven foot Airstream Classic and he was looking for a quick sale. Wanted ten thousand for it.

"It was a steal at that price. We had him give us directions and we drove over to take a look. We couldn't get inside, but it looked to be in good shape so we called him and said we'd buy it. He said he'd sell it to us if we brought the money to him in Crystal River."

Devin stopped him. "Crystal River? That's where he

lives? Crystal River?"

"Yeah, Crystal River. We met him in the parking lot of the bank there."

Devin wasn't smiling. "What did he look like, this guy you bought the trailer from?"

Dabbo thought about it then said, "Short, stocky, with red hair. Dressed like a banker."

"What was his name?"

Dabbo looked up and squinted like he was trying to remember. Apparently it helped. "Fowler. That's his name. Martin Fowler. Check the bill of sale. That's how he signed it."

Devin didn't bother to check, instead she asked, "Did he have a mark on his face? On his cheek?"

"Yeah, he did. On the left side. A red splotch, shaped kind of like Florida."

Devin shook her head in disgust. "That bastard. Somehow he found out who I was and did this to me."

Dabbo didn't understand what she was talking about, but Kat and I did. We knew about the man Devin had met back at the dollar store in Crystal River. She had tricked him into paying her because he'd gotten her pregnant.

But the pregnancy wasn't real, and apparently Fowler had figured out a way to get his money back. By selling her trailer to Dabbo and his friends.

Devin turned to Dabbo. "When did this happen? When did the guy call you about buying my trailer?"

"Last week, Sunday I think. We went to see the trailer on Monday, and went to Crystal River on Tuesday to pay for it. On Wednesday we had the Trailer Monkeys tow it away."

She turned to Kat. "Fowler must have planned this ahead of time. He knew I was still in Crystal River last week. He planned it so he'd have the money to pay me off and my trailer would be gone when I got back to Niceville.

"He must have hired someone to find out about me. This really sucks."

She turned back to Dabbo. "Where's my trailer now?"

He shrugged. "We don't know. The Trailer Monkeys were supposed to bring it to our shop but they never showed up.

"We tried calling them, but they never answer. When we saw Pico getting lunch on Thursday, we tried to get some answers from him but your friend over there stopped us."

Devin nodded. "Sorry about that. We didn't know what was going on. We thought Pico was in trouble and needed help."

"Yeah, I can see how it might have looked that way. So no harm done. But just so you know, we wouldn't have hurt him. Not bad anyway. We just wanted to know what happened to the trailer we'd paid ten thousand dollars for. Speaking of which, how do we get our money back?"

Devin gave him a quick answer. "Find my trailer then we'll talk about money. Not until then."

She turned to me. "We need to find Pico and Squally. They'll know where my trailer is."

The Monte Carlo was sitting between us and the mud hole. We weren't going to get past it until it was moved.

I turned to Dabbo. "I'm going to back up to that wide spot in the road behind me. That'll give you room to get past. Then I'm going through the mud again. I'll wait for you on the other side to pull you out. That work for you?"

Dabbo nodded. "Yeah, that'll work."

I backed up and let Dabbo get his Monte Carlo past us. Then, with the girls in the back seat, I lined up for another run at the hole. There wasn't as much mud as there had been before. We'd pulled a lot of it out with the Monte Carlo.

I was doing thirty when I hit the mud. Not as fast as when Devin hit it but we sailed across with no problem. I parked on the other side and waited for Dabbo to make his run.

He got the Monte Carlo up to speed and the hit the hole full bore. The mud tore the plastic front bumper off soon after, but Dabbo didn't let up until he was up on dry ground on the other side. Steam was coming from under the car's hood, but he'd made it across without our help.

He pulled up behind the Bronco and got out to talk. He started out by saying, "We didn't know it was McSweeney's Airstream. We wouldn't have bought it if we did. Tell her we'll help her get it back. But she's got to promise not to get us in trouble with her father. And it'd be nice if she could help get our money back. Or at least some of it."

I nodded. "I don't know about the money, but if you help her find the trailer, she won't tell her father. If we don't find the trailer or if it's wrecked, all bets are off."

Dabbo nodded. "We'll find it. We'll get our people looking for it."

He put out his hand to shake. "Sorry about last night. We wouldn't have jumped you if we'd known what was going on."

I shook and we traded phone numbers. Dabbo said he'd call as soon as he learned anything. I didn't tell him we'd heard Pico and Squally were hiding out in St. Joe. That was a lead we were going to follow up on our own, starting with a records search as soon as we got back to the motorhome.

Chapter Forty

We'd wasted most of the morning on a wild goose chase on Dry Bones Road, thanks to Brandi. We didn't need to waste any more time. What we needed to do was find Devin's trailer.

Leaving the mud hole behind, we got back on 98 and headed west toward St. Joe. Devin was driving, Kat was in the passenger seat and I was in the back. Neither of them had said much since we'd hit 98. I figured Devin was thinking about how she had been conned by the man in Crystal River. A man she thought she was conning.

Turned out he knew about her scheme, knew she wasn't under age, and probably knew she wasn't really pregnant. He'd agreed to pay her cash to go away. But it looked like he'd gotten the cash by selling Devin's Airstream to Dabbo and his two buddies.

She finally spoke up. "I can't call the cops on Fowler. If I do, he'll tell them I was blackmailing him. Whether they believe him or not won't matter. They'll put my name in the system and it'll go downhill from there. In the meantime, whoever has the trailer will have plenty of time to take it north and make it disappear. We need to find it before that happens."

Neither Kat nor I said anything. We pretty much agreed with what Devin had said. There wasn't anything we could say that would make her feel better or help us find the trailer faster.

We were almost to St. Joe when I made a suggestion. "Let's stop at the barbeque place again. I want to talk to the lady there, see if she's seen Pico. Maybe he's been back."

Devin wasn't so sure. "After the beating he got there, he won't go back. He's not a fool."

"You're probably right. But it doesn't hurt to ask. Maybe he's a regular and they know where he lives. Even if they don't know anything, we can pick up lunch."

She kept driving. Ten minutes later, she pulled into the barbeque lot. Not much had changed since the last time we'd been there. They were serving food out the same trailer and the same woman who'd taken my order the day before was still working the window.

Kat and Devin wanted pork sandwiches and iced tea. I decided to get the same. I walked up and placed my order. After the woman had written it down I asked, "Did you see the fight in the parking lot yesterday?"

She nodded. "You mean when Pico got jumped?"

"Yeah, you saw that?"

"Sure did. Was about to call the cops, but it was over and everybody left. Even the guys with the flat tires."

"So is Pico okay?"

She shook her head. "Don't know. I haven't seen him since. You a friend of his?"

"Yes ma'am, I am. I've got a trailer I need moved and can't seem to find him."

"You try calling?"

"I did, but the number I have is out of service. He have a new number?"

She shrugged. "Don't know. Never had the need to call

214

him. Check his website, the number there ought to be good."

She nodded her head toward the back and disappeared to make our sandwiches. While waiting for her to return, I sat down in one of the metal chairs under the awning to the right of the order window. My ribs still hurt from the punches I'd taken from Dabbo and his buddies. Sitting felt better than standing.

As I sat there, I tried to remember everything I could about the fight from the day before. The Trailer Monkey truck had shown up after I'd gotten back in the motorhome with our food. We saw Pico place his order. It didn't look like anyone was in the truck with him.

Dabbo and his buddies in the blue Monte Carlo were going west on 98 when they saw Pico's truck and pulled in. When the fight was over, Pico left the parking lot using the entrance that bordered 98 and headed west.

Kat had taken us out of the back entrance into a residential area. Two minutes later, we were on 98, going west, just like Pico. But we never saw his truck, either in front or behind us. With the Monkeys on the door, it would have been hard to miss.

He couldn't have gotten too far ahead of us, not in his tow truck. There wasn't much traffic on 98 and we should have caught up with him sooner or later. But we hadn't.

When we stopped for the rainstorm, he wasn't behind us. At least not close enough for us to see. There'd been enough stop and go traffic going through Mexico Beach for him to catch up if he'd been behind us.

The only way it made sense for us not to have seen him on 98 was if he turned off in St. Joe almost as soon as he got on it. If he did that, it could mean he was staying somewhere in St. Joe, like Brandi had said.

Behind me I heard, "Your order's ready."

I paid the lady, thanked her for her help, and took the food back to the Bronco. Devin said she didn't want us spilling barbeque on her seats so the food stayed in the bag for the five minutes it took for us to get back to our site in the Indian Pass RV Park.

For me, it was like coming home. Bob met me at the door and was happy to see me. He was purring loudly and showed his affection by wrapping his body around my feet. I reached down and petted him on the head and said, "Bob, you're a good kitty."

The smell of the barbeque in the bag I was carrying got his attention. He stood up on his hind legs and sniffed the bag. He reached out to touch it with his paw, but before he could get to it, I lifted the bag above his head and said, "No, Bob. This is not for you."

He huffed his displeasure then walked over to Kat. He rubbed her ankles hoping she would pet him. She did. He looked back at me, as to say, "At least she still likes me," and then he trotted back to the bedroom for his afternoon nap. He'd totally ignored Devin. It didn't seem to bother her though. She had other things on her mind.

After we took turns washing up, we put the food out and ate. Mostly in silence.

I finished my sandwich first and said, "We should have called the Trailer Monkeys as soon as we found out they were the ones who towed it away. Kat should call since she knows Pico and Squally the best."

She agreed. "I'll call them, but I don't know if they'll talk to me."

She looked up their number on the web and made the call. She put her phone on speaker so we could hear what

216

was said.

After six rings, a woman's voice came on and said, "Sorry, the Trailer Monkeys are not able to come to the phone right now. Please try again later." The call ended without giving the option to leave a message.

Kat looked up and asked, "Now what?"

Chapter Forty-one

I got up from the table, went back to the bedroom and grabbed my laptop from the top shelf of my closet. It'd been almost a week since I'd last used it, but I'd put it away with a full charge. I was pretty sure it was ready to go.

The RV park had free Wi-Fi and, using the password they'd given me when I checked in, I was able to get onto the net. Sitting across from Kat and Devin at the kitchen table with the laptop on in front of me, I asked, "What's Pico's last name?"

Kat answered first. "Gaines. Pico Gaines."

"Is Pico his real name?"

Kat nodded. "I think so."

"How about Squally? That his real name?"

"Yeah, it is. He told me his mother was a fan of the Weather Channel. When she was pregnant she heard them talking about 'squally' weather in the forecast and she liked the way the word sounded. So that's what she named him. Squally.

"I think Pico is something in the metric system. They used it on the Weather Channel once and that's what she named her second boy. So yeah, they're their real names. Pico and Squally Gaines."

While she was telling me this, I'd started a public records search for Pico Gaines. First, a property search to see if he owned any property in Apalachicola or Port St. Joe. Nothing turned up.

Then I did an arrest records search. It probably wouldn't show me his home address but might give some insight into what he was up to. As before, nothing showed up. He was clean.

I followed this with a DMV search. Vehicles registered in his name would show up and might include a home address. This time, the search showed seven vehicles over the past ten years registered to a Pico Gaines. Unfortunately, none were current registrations. No addresses were listed for any of the vehicles.

Next up was a marriage license search. Again, no matches found. I followed this with a court records search, a death certificate search, and then finally a Facebook search.

Again nothing. Pico had done a good job of staying off the web. I did the same sequence of searches for Squally Gaines. This time, I hit pay dirt.

"Kat, did you know Squally got married?"

She looked at me in disbelief. "He got married? Squally got married? Are you sure?"

I looked at the record on the screen. "Yeah, it says here that Squally Gaines of Port St. Joe Florida got married. June of last year. To Ashley Jordan Peale."

After she caught her breath, Kat looked at me shaking her head. "Are you kidding me? Ashley married Squally? That's unbelievable! I never thought she'd go back to him. I'd sure like to know how that happened."

Devin nodded. "Me too. What else does it say?"

I scanned the page. "No home address, but the license was issued in Gulf County, Florida."

"What about pictures? Are there any pictures of Ashley?

Was she pregnant?"

Before I could answer, Kat's phone began playing the Darth Vader ring tone. She held a finger to her lips. "Be quiet, it's my dad."

"Hi Daddy."

"No, we haven't got there yet. We decided to spend a day in Apalachicola.

"The three of us. Me, Devin, and Walker.

"Yes, he's been a perfect gentleman.

"I'll tell him you said that, but you really wouldn't, would you?

"Okay, as soon as we pick it up, I'll call you.

"I promise. Bye."

She ended the call and smiled at me. "Daddy was checking up on us. He was wondering why we haven't picked up the package and why I hadn't called him about it.

"He said the package was very important and not to lose it. He said to call him as soon as I have it in my hands."

I was waiting for her to tell me more about the conversation, especially the part that seemed to be about me. But she didn't. She acted like that was all there was to it.

I decided to press her. "So, did he ask about me?"

She nodded. "He did. I told him you were a perfect gentleman."

"I heard that part. But what about when you asked if he really would do something to me. What was that about?"

She smiled. "Nothing to worry about. As long as you stay on my good side, he promised he wouldn't castrate you."

"Well, that's reassuring."

"Really, I won't let him do anything to you. But you might want to think twice before you go out with Brandi tonight."

When I heard the word 'castrate', I'd already decided. No dinner with Brandi.

I turned back to my computer. "You were asking about wedding photos. Let me see if I can find some."

I did a search on Google but had no luck there. I went back to Facebook and searched for Ashley Jordan Peale. There were seven of them, including one from Port St. Joe. I brought up her page and turned the laptop around so Kat could see.

"That's her! That's her picture."

She pointed to the screen and turned it so Devin could see. I wasn't interested in the pictures unless they could help me find Devin's trailer. I doubted they would.

So far, my internet search hadn't given us a street address for Pico or Squally. But we'd learned Squally had gotten married in Port St. Joe. That little bit of information gave me hope he was still living close by.

As the girls scanned Ashley's Facebook page, a thought came to me. Brandi had said Pico was probably laying low at his brother's place in St. Joe. We hadn't had much luck in finding a St. Joe address for Squally. But what if she meant his brother-in-law?

Since Squally had gotten married, maybe he now had a brother-in-law. Maybe the brother-in-law had a place in St. Joe. I asked Kat. "Does Ashley have a brother?"

She thought for a moment. "Yeah, she does. His name is Brock. Built like a rock, Brock. That's what we used to say about him."

"Good, let me see the computer."

She slid it over to me and I started a new property search. This time for Brock Peale. Ashley's brother.

Chapter Forty-two

"Bingo! Found him. Says here he has a place on Marvin Avenue in St. Joe."

The property search for Brock Peale, Squally's new brother-in-law, had paid off. I'd found a home he owned in St. Joe. We looked up the address using Google maps and saw that it was just a few miles from our campsite. Devin grabbed the keys to the Bronco and said, "Let's go see if he's there."

We headed north on 98, turned right on Sixteenth Street and then made another right onto Marvin Avenue. The third house down was Brock's. Single story ranch, two cars and a motorcycle in the driveway. Freshly mowed lawn.

Devin parked in front of the house. She started to get out, but I stopped her. "Let me go knock on the door. If Pico's there, maybe he'll remember I helped in the parking lot fight. Be good if he did."

Devin didn't object, so I got out and walked up to the door. I rang the doorbell and almost immediately heard a woman's voice say, "Boy, get up and go see who's at the door."

A moment later, a teenaged boy opened the door. "You selling something?"

I shook my head. "No, I'm looking for Pico. Or Squally. Thought they might be here."

The boy looked over his shoulder and yelled, "Mom, come talk to this guy." Then he walked away.

I stood at the open door waiting for his mother. I didn't know what to expect but I figured a smile might help. It didn't.

A middle-aged woman, a little on the heavy side, wearing shorts and a T-shirt walked up and said, "What do you want?"

"I'm looking for Pico or Squally."

"What makes you think either one of them would be here?"

"Pico said to look for him here. I owe him some money and want to pay up. If he's not here, I leave. Don't want to waste your time."

I started to turn and walk away, but the woman stopped me.

"Wait! You got money for Pico? How much?"

I turned and walked back to the door.

"Six hundred dollars. For moving that Airstream two days ago."

She shook her head. "That ain't enough for all the trouble that thing's caused. It's going to take more."

She leaned in to get a closer look at my face. "You been in a fight?"

"Yes ma'am, I have. I saw Pico get jumped by three guys at the barbeque place yesterday. I pulled them off him. Last night, those same three guys caught up with me and got some payback."

She looked at me. "So you was the one who helped him the other day?"

"Yes ma'am. That was me. I sprayed those guys with a fire extinguisher. Ask Pico."

"I don't need to ask him. He told me all about it. Said you saved him from a pretty good beating. That was good of you."

"Now, about that money, you'll need more than six hundred dollars to pay for the trouble that Airstream has caused. But maybe Pico will discount it a bit since you helped him out."

I smiled. "That'd be good of him. Would it be alright if I paid him today? I got the money with me and I'd pay if I can get the trailer back. Is he around? I'd like to talk to him about it."

She looked at me like she was sizing me up. Deciding whether she should tell me where Pico was or send me on my way. I knew she wanted the money, but she also wanted to protect Pico. I smiled at her. Hoping that'd sway her a bit in my direction. Apparently it did. She said, "Wait here. Don't go nowhere."

She turned around and shouted, "Pico, there's a man here wants to give you some money. Come talk to him."

A few minutes later, a man came to the door. His face had the same kind of bruises I had. Eyes swollen with dark circles. His first words were, "So they caught up with you, huh?"

"Yeah, last night. Hurts like hell. How about you?"

He shrugged. "Ribs hurt the most. Don't think anything's broken though."

"Yeah, mine hurt too. But I've settled things with them. They've got no reason to hurt you now."

"Good. But why'd you get involved in the first place?"

I pointed over my shoulder to the Bronco. "Kat and Devin. Friends of yours from way back. They saw the guys jump you and sent me in to make it an even fight."

227

He looked over my shoulder. "Kat and Devin are here? With you? Really? I haven't seen them in years. How they doing?"

"Pretty good. You want to talk to them? They kind of need your help."

"Yeah, I want to talk to them. But I got to put shoes on before I go out there. There's stickers in the grass."

He went back in the house, leaving me standing at the open door. I wasn't going to go inside without permission, so I turned and gave the girls a thumbs up. Things were looking good.

When Pico returned, we walked out to the Bronco. About half way there, the girls got out to meet us. Kat ran up and gave him a hug. "Pico, it's been a long time."

He nodded. "It sure has."

Devin reached out to shake his hand. "Pico."

He looked at her, grabbed her hand and pulled her in for a hug. "Devin, you're looking mighty fine."

She pushed him away. "Where's my trailer?"

"Your trailer? What makes you think I know anything about your trailer? I didn't even know you had a trailer."

She crossed her arms. "That Airstream trailer you picked up three days ago, it was mine. The people who sold it didn't own it. I want it back."

Pico thought for a moment then said, "Maybe that's why they're holding him."

"Holding who?"

"Squally. They arrested him when we were bringing the trailer back. We got caught up in a rainstorm and slid off the road. Someone called the sheriff and next thing I know they

228

put Squally in the patrol car and impounded the trailer. They let me keep the tow truck, but they kept Squally.

"They wouldn't tell me why they were taking him or why they impounded the trailer. They just said something about the VIN not matching the tow order. I showed them the copy of the bill of sale and they said that didn't match the VIN either. They said they'd be holding the trailer until things got settled.

"Far as I know, it's still in the impound lot. Maybe if you show up with a title with the right VIN and enough money, they'll release it to you. Course, you might need someone to haul it back to Niceville. I'll be glad to do it for you. Even give you a discount."

Devin shook her head. "You're telling me my trailer is sitting in an impound lot and all I need to do to get it is to go over there and bail it out?"

Pico nodded. "Yeah, if you go over there during business hours, show up with a valid driver's license and paperwork showing the trailer is yours, you can get it. You will have to pay the three hundred dollar tow fee and the hundred-dollar-a-day impound fee. Once you pay, you can haul it away.

"The thing is, it's not at the impound lot here in St. Joe. It's in the Tow Rite lot in Panama City. Normally, the county would call us for their tow jobs, and we'd take it to the St. Joe lot. But since it was one of us they were arresting, they had to call Tow Rite. They took it to their lot in PC.

"I can go over there with you in my tow truck and haul it back to Niceville. We could do it in the morning if you wanted to. I'll waive the normal tow fee if you pay for my gas over there and back."

Devin thought for a moment then said, "Why can't we do

it today? Why can't we go there right now?"

Pico had a quick answer. "Because Tow Rite closes their lot at six. No way we'd get over there in time. You got the title on you? Because, no matter when we get there, they won't release it without seeing the title."

Devin shook her head. "The title is locked up inside the trailer. Will they let me go in and get it?

"No, they won't let you get near the trailer until you show them proof of ownership. But if the trailer is registered to you, you can go online and get what you need from the Florida DMV site. Just show Tow Rite the DMV printout, pay their tow and lot fees and they'll let you take it."

Pico looked over his shoulder to the house then, in a near whisper, he said, "Before we go over to PC, we ought to get Squally out. He's sitting in the county lockup, just down the road from here. We could go over there right now. You could talk to the sheriff, tell him you're the owner of the trailer and they might let us bond him out."

Devin didn't seem too keen on what Pico had suggested. She asked, "Why would I want to do that? Seems like it's because of Squally I'm in this mess. If you want him out so bad, why don't you go down there and pay his bond?"

Pico again looked over his shoulder to make sure no one from the house was listening. "Here's the thing. Money is kind of tight around here right now. With Ashley expecting again, she and Squally are a little behind on their bills. She can't really afford to spend that kind of money, not with another baby on the way.

"I can't cover it either. But if you were to go down there and talk to the sheriff, they might reduce Squally's bond. If you clear up the VIN problem, the sheriff might even call Tow Rite and authorize them to release the trailer to you."

Devin's expression changed. "You said the jail is close?"

"Yeah, about a mile from here. We could be over there in a couple of minutes. What do you say? Will you do it?"

"Yeah, I'll go over there. But only because it might help me get my trailer back. I'm not paying anything to get Squally out. That's something you'll have to deal with."

Pico smiled. "That's fine with me. Give me five minutes to change into decent clothes and we'll go over there." He ran back toward the house, presumably to change clothes.

When we got back in the Bronco, Kat asked me, "If Squally is in jail, why didn't it show up on your search?"

It was a good question but an easy one to answer. "According to Pico, they arrested him two days ago. They probably haven't entered it into the system yet. Or maybe they haven't filed any charges. Whatever the reason, I wouldn't ask about it when we get over there. Just let Devin tell her story, see what happens."

When Pico came back out, he was wearing long pants, a clean, white shirt and carrying a manila folder. He walked up to the Bronco and started to get in the backseat.

Kat stopped him. "You have a car?"

"Yeah, the green Dodge over there."

"Is it legal? Got tags and insurance?"

"Yeah, why?"

"I think it'd be better if you took it. That way Squally can ride back with you. There's not enough room in here for all of us."

Pico looked at the Bronco. There was plenty of room. He could see that. But he didn't say anything. He didn't need to start a fight with Kat. He knew it wouldn't help him get Squally out of jail. "Separate cars. Good idea. I'll go get my keys and you can follow me over there."

He went back in the house. While we waited for him to come back out, Devin looked at Kat. "You don't want Squally riding with us?"

Kat didn't answer. She didn't have to. Squally had married Ashley after dumping Kat. Having him ride in the crowded Bronco with us would make for a very uncomfortable reunion.

Chapter Forty-three

It didn't take long to get to the sheriff's office. Pico was right; it was just a few blocks away. On the ride over, Kat said she wouldn't be going in. She was going to wait outside in the Bronco. Devin didn't have a problem with that. But when I said I'd go in with her and meet the sheriff, she said, "No. You stay out in the car with Kat."

"Why? Why can't I go in with you?" I asked.

"Because if you go in there with all those bruises on your face, the sheriff's liable to ask questions. The kind you really don't want to answer. So it'd be better if you stayed outside."

She was probably right. If I went in there looking all beat up, standing alongside Pico who also looked like he'd been in a fight, there'd be questions. There wasn't any way the answers were going to help get Squally or get Devin's trailer back. It made sense for me to stay outside with Kat.

When we got to the sheriff's office, Devin parked in the shade of a tree near the front door. She grabbed a wallet out of the duffel that had been my backseat companion for the past two days. I assumed the wallet was where she kept her driver's license and cash.

"Wish me luck," she said as she followed Pico inside.

As planned, Kat and I stayed out in the Bronco. Devin had left the keys in the ignition in case we needed to start the engine and run the air conditioner. In the shade with the windows down we didn't need to. At least not right away.

Kat didn't seem to be in a talkative mood, but I was. "Think I should call Dabbo, let him know we found Pico and Squally?"

She shrugged. "If you want to."

I did. Dabbo answered on the third ring.

"Yeah, this is Dabbo."

"It's me, Walker. You can call off the search. We found Pico and Squally. We know were the trailer is."

"That's good. We been looking for them all over town and hadn't had any luck. Where'd you find them?"

"In jail. They got Squally on suspicion of transporting stolen property. Something about the VIN not matching the tow order on the trailer."

"Really? The VIN doesn't match? Does that mean I'm going to be in trouble for ordering the tow?"

"Probably not. The McSweeney girl is in there with the sheriff. Trying to smooth things over. If it works out, she'll get her trailer back. That'll be the end of it."

Dabbo was relieved. "Hope it works out for her. But what about me?"

"What do you mean what about you?"

"The money. I paid a lot of money for the trailer. More than I can afford to lose. Think there's any way I can get it back?"

I didn't know the answer, so I asked him a question. "How much did you pay for the trailer? I know you didn't pay full price. So be honest, how much did you pay?"

Dabbo took a deep breath then said, "The guy was asking ten grand. But when we met up with him, I was able to bargain him down to eight. I paid him in cash, hundred

234

dollar bills. I paid another three hundred to the Trailer Monkeys to move it.

"I'm out eight thousand three hundred, not including what it cost to drive to Crystal River and Niceville. Like I said, I can't afford to lose that kind of money."

It was a lot of money to lose, especially for a small time operator like Dabbo. I needed to talk to Devin, see if I could figure a way to get some of his money back. But I didn't have high hopes.

"Dabbo, I don't figure you're going to get your gas money back. And I doubt the Trailer Monkeys are going to give you a refund. You might as well write that money off as the cost of doing business.

"But there is a slight chance I might be able to convince Devin to help you out with some of what you lost. I can't guarantee she'll go for it. But I'll talk to her. I'll call you when I know something."

I ended the call.

From the front seat, Kat said, "You shouldn't get his hopes up. No way Devin is going to give him any of his money back."

I nodded. "You're probably right. But it might be in her best interest to keep Dabbo happy. She won't want him to go to the police. It could come back on her."

Kat shrugged like she didn't care. Then she said, "It's hot in here." She started the Bronco, turned on the air, and rolled up the windows. A minute later, I could feel the waves of chilled air crossing into the backseat where I was sitting, each one trying to chase away the heat that had built up while we waited for Devin's return.

Five minutes later, Kat said, "Here they come."

Looking out the window, I saw Devin, followed by Pico and another man. Most likely Squally. Long, greasy hair, unshaven, dirty and wrinkled clothes. Big grin on his face. Clearly happy to be out of lockup.

The three of them stopped in front of the Bronco. Over the sound of the AC, I heard Devin tell Pico she'd be at his place in the morning. She was saying, "I expect you and your truck to be ready. I want you to drive, not Squally.

"I'll follow you all the way there in the Bronco. You'll get my trailer and take it back to my place in Niceville. No mistakes this time. Make sure you have plenty of gas in your truck before you leave."

Pico was nodding his head at everything she was saying, trying to show he was paying attention. But not Squally, he quickly lost interest and walked over to the Bronco's passenger door. He tapped on the window to get Kat's attention. She was leaned over in her seat, head down under the dash, pretending she was looking for something on the floor. She didn't bother looking up. She knew who was tapping on the glass and she had no intention of talking to him.

He tapped again and said, "Kat, roll down your window."

She sat up, turned around and looked at me. "You see that fool out there? Do me a favor. See if you can get him to go away."

I didn't know what it would take to get Squally to leave, but I figured I'd try a few things. I opened the back door and climbed out. I stood up straight, towering about four inches above his head. That got his attention.

I smiled and said, "Squally, let's go over there by that bench and talk. Kat has something she wants me to tell you."

He looked at Kat sitting in the passenger seat. "Why can't

she tell me herself?"

I shrugged. "You know how women are. Come on, let's go over there and talk."

I started to walk away, seeing if Squally would follow me. He did.

When we got to the bench, I stuck out my hand and introduced myself. "Hi, I'm Walker."

Squally shook my hand. "Okay, Walker. What you want to talk about?"

I nodded toward Kat in the Bronco. "It's like this. Me and Kat, we're together, if you know what I mean. Kind of like husband and wife. But we don't want Devin to know. So I'm trusting you won't tell her.

"I'm also trusting you won't be bothering Kat because, if you do, then I have to get involved. You probably won't like that."

Squally looked at me. "How'd you get that cut on your face? And the bruises? You in a fight?"

"Yeah, I was. Me against three. They didn't have a chance. Ask Pico. He knows about it."

Squally looked back to where Pico was standing. In front of Devin, listening to whatever she was still talking to him about.

He looked back at me. "You a tough guy?"

I smiled and in a low voice I said, "I might be. There's one sure way for you to find out. Just bother Kat again. See what happens."

Squally didn't ask any more questions. He just stood there, sizing me up and mulling over his options. He probably didn't want to fight. Too many reasons not to. He'd just been bailed out of jail and was standing in the sheriff's office parking lot. If he threw a punch, he might be spending the night behind bars again.

Then again, maybe he was thinking if he took me on, Kat would be impressed. Maybe to him that was worth the risk of another night or two in jail.

Fortunately, Pico saw what was happening and called out. "Squally, come back over here. You're in enough trouble as it. Don't get in any more."

Squally looked at me, leaned in and whispered, "Tell her I'm sorry." Then he walked over to Pico's car and got in on the passenger side. Pico joined him and they drove off.

Devin, who was still standing outside the Bronco, watched as they left. She shook her head and walked over. "I saw you talking to him. What was that about?"

"Just me getting to know him. That's all."

I didn't think she believed me but it didn't matter because she didn't ask any follow up questions. She pointed at the Bronco and said, "Let's go."

As soon as I got in the back seat, Kat turned to me and said, "Thank you." Then she turned to Devin and asked, "How'd it go in there with the Sheriff?"

Devin smiled. "Much better than I expected. After I showed him my driver's license and he confirmed I was the owner of the Airstream, he called the impound yard and gave them a release authorization. I can pick it up tomorrow.

"As for Squally, the sheriff was happy to get rid of him. He was taking up valuable jail space and bothering his cell mates. I paid off a couple of his parking tickets and they let him go. He'll still have to get his license renewed and pay a fine, but that's not something we have to worry about.

"I'm going over to Panama City in the morning to get the

trailer. Pico will haul it back to Niceville and put it back the way it was. If all goes well, this thing will be over tomorrow."

She put the Bronco in gear and we headed back toward town. We'd gone about a mile when she said, "I need to get gas before I drive to Niceville in the morning. Mind if I stop and do it now?"

There were no objections. She headed to the Exxon station on 98, the one next to Burger King. When she stopped at the pump, I got out to stretch and to help her with the gas. As I reached for the nozzle, she slapped my hand and said, "I can do it."

I smiled. "I know you can, but it feels good when I help. Let me do it for you."

She frowned and said, "Men. You're nothing but trouble."

She was probably right. But she didn't stop me from pumping the gas.

With the tank full, I took my place in the back seat and waited for Devin. I still wanted to talk to her about Dabbo and the money but this clearly wasn't the right time. Not now, with her thinking men were nothing but trouble.

As soon as we got back on the road, Kat said, "I think we need some wine. Where's the closest place we can we get some?"

I remembered seeing a liquor store at the north end of town, not far from the Exxon station. "Up ahead on the right. Pull in and I'll get it."

When we reached the store, Devin pulled in and parked. I got out and went inside. The girls stayed in the Bronco and talked. The liquor store was small but well stocked. I went to the cooler in the back and grabbed two bottles of Lindeman's Chardonnay. Not expensive, but I knew Kat liked this brand. From behind me, I heard her voice. She said, "That won't be enough. Better get two more of those. I'm thirsty."

I was happy to oblige. I picked up a bottle caddy from the stack near the cooler and filled all four slots with cold Chardonnay. I figured four would be more than enough for the three of us, especially since I didn't plan to drink.

Kat wanted more. Something she could start with in the car. She grabbed a four pack of airline size wine bottles from the cooler and met me at the checkout counter. I pulled out my credit card and paid for what would turn out to be our night's entertainment.

Back outside, Devin had gotten out of the driver's seat and moved into the back where I'd been sitting. She handed me the keys and said, "You drive."

After getting the Bronco back out on the road, I started thinking about the evening ahead. I knew that once we got back to the motorhome and the girls started drinking, they'd want something to eat. They wouldn't want to drink on an empty stomach.

I also knew we didn't have much food left in the fridge and I wouldn't want to go back out and get some later. Now was the time to do it, while everyone was still sober. So I asked, "What do you girls want to eat tonight?"

Devin answered first. "Anything but barbeque. We had that for lunch. Whatever you get, it's got to be takeout. I don't want to go into a restaurant and wait an hour for food. I want it to be quick so we can go home and celebrate."

Kat agreed. "Get something fast and take us home. Think you can do that?"

I was pretty sure I could. The Piggly Wiggly was just ahead and I pulled in and parked. I handed my phone to Devin and said, "Call Dabbo. Talk to him about the eight thousand dollars he's out."

I didn't wait to see what she'd say. I grabbed the keys and went in. Kat could fill Devin in on the conversation I'd had with Dabbo while she was in the sheriff's office.

Inside the Piggly Wiggly, I got a cart and loaded it up with drinking food. Two bags of pretzels, two boxes of crackers, a bag of sliced pepper jack cheese and a second bag of extra sharp. In the deli, I got a pound of sliced turkey and three pounds of cooked chicken wings. And just in case this wasn't enough, I headed over to the frozen foods section and grabbed two frozen pizzas.

On the way to the checkout stand, I remembered coffee and grabbed a box of Starbucks Instant. I didn't know what kind of coffee Kat preferred, but I figured Starbucks would keep her from complaining to me about not having any coffee in the motorhome.

I paid for everything and headed back outside. I put the food in the back next to Devin. She and Kat had gotten into the wine. Each had opened one of the little bottles and was doing a good job of emptying them. They offered me one but, since I was driving, I'd had to say, "No."

It was a relief when we finally pulled up in front of the motorhome at the RV park. It'd been a long day. But worth it. We'd found Devin's trailer. And that was all that really mattered.

At least, that's what I thought.

Chapter Forty-four

As usual, Bob met us at the door. He was happy we were back and I was particularly happy to see him. Me being gone two or three days in a row wasn't something he was used to. He liked things to stay the same. I did too.

This little road trip with Kat and Devin had already lasted a lot longer than it should have, and it wasn't over yet. Both Bob and I were looking forward to getting back to our normal routine. But first we had to get through the night.

I unpacked the food, brought out the wine glasses and put an open bottle on the table. Kat poured a glass for each of us and we toasted finding Devin's trailer.

While the girls finished off their wine, I got plates and napkins from the kitchen pantry and put pretzels and chicken wings on the table in front of them. I was doing my best to be the perfect host, while trying not to be obvious about not drinking glass for glass with the girls. I'd been down that road before and it was a contest I couldn't win. Instead of drinking with them, I plied them with food. It seemed to work.

After they finished the first bottle, I opened the second and refilled their glasses. They didn't seem to notice or care that I didn't fill mine.

About an hour later, I heard a car pull up outside followed by the sound of a car door being opened then shut. A few seconds later, there was a knock at our door. We definitely weren't expecting visitors. No one was supposed to know we were there.

I was afraid that it could be the local sheriff coming to pick up Devin or Kat or maybe even me. Because I was the only one sober, I went to check.

It wasn't the sheriff. It was Dabbo. His blue Monte Carlo was parked behind the Bronco and he was standing in front of it. His two sidekicks were in the car behind him. They had their windows rolled down so they could hear what was being said.

I played nice. "Dabbo, surprised to see you here. How'd you find us?"

"Devin called me. Said to meet her here around seven. She inside?"

I nodded but I didn't feel like inviting him in. It wasn't that I didn't like him, just that, after taking a beating from him the night before, I wasn't feeling real cordial.

"Let me go inside and check."

I went inside, closing the door behind me, and walked over to Devin. "Dabbo's outside. Says you told him to meet you here."

With a glass of wine in one hand and a chicken wing in the other, she said, "That's what I told him. I'm giving him back the eight thousand he paid for the trailer. In return, he promised not to go to the police and not to go after Fowler."

She pulled a thick white envelope from her back pocket and slid it across the table to me. "Give this to Dabbo. Remind him of our deal."

I looked at the thick envelope, presumably filled with money. It was sealed, so I didn't know for sure. I wondered if Devin would regret this in the morning, especially considering how much she'd already had to drink.

"Are you sure you want to do this? Now?"

"Yeah, I'm sure. Just give it to him."

She took a drink, pointed her finger at me and slurred. "Hurry, 'cause when you come back, I got a question for you."

Giving Dabbo back his money was the right thing to do. But I was surprised Devin gave it up so easily. Maybe she understood that giving the money back took care of what might otherwise have been a long-term problem. I picked up the envelope and took it outside.

I showed it to Dabbo and said, "Devin said to remind you about the deal she made with you. Don't go to the police and don't go after the guy in Crystal River. Understood?"

"Yeah, I understand. Tell her if she needs me again to call. It was a pleasure doing business with her. Same goes for you."

I handed him the envelope. He put it in his back pocket without bothering to open it or counting the money. He must have been a trusting sort of person. I wouldn't have been. I would have counted it.

He stuck out his hand. "We good?"

"Yeah. We're good."

He got back in his car and drove off. As he was leaving, I was hoping it was going to be the last time I saw the blue Monte Carlo and the people in it. Dabbo turned out to be a good guy, but it could have easily gone a different way.

Back inside, Devin waved me over to the table. She reached out for my arm and said, "I have a problem that I need your help with."

She took a drink from her now almost empty glass then continued. She spoke slowly, fighting the effects of the wine, trying hard to get the words out in the right order. "Pico is going to follow me to the impound yard in Panama City in the morning. I'll going to bail out my trailer and then he's going to tow it back to Niceville. He's going to put it back the way he found it."

She took a deep breath. "Here's the problem.

"The package I'm supposed to give Kat is in my trailer. When I get to the impound yard, I'll get it out and give it to her. But after I do that, I'm going home with my trailer. I'm not coming back to St. Joe.

"If the two of you ride over there with me in the Bronco, you'll need to figure out a way to get back here on your own.

"You might be able to catch a ride with Pico and Squally in their tow truck."

She had more to say but Kat interrupted her. "No way I'd riding with Squally in a tow truck. Not for a mile and certainly not for a hundred. That's not going to happen."

She looked at me. "Walker dear, would you drive me over to Panama City in your motorhome in the morning? It'd really make me happy if you would."

I knew the right answer to the question. "Kat, any excuse to spend more time with you pleases me to no end. So yes, I'll be more than happy to drive you over there."

The truth of the matter was, if driving her to Panama City made her happy and got this trip over with, I was all for it. Of course, that's not exactly what I told her. But she was happy with the answer I gave.

She leaned in and kissed me on the cheek. "Walker, you say the nicest things."

After that, the night was mostly the girls drinking wine, eating chicken wings and me heating up cheese and turkey on crackers in the microwave.

The cracker snacks went over well as did the chicken wings and pretzels. We never got to the pizza. After finishing off two and a half bottles of wine between them, the girls were ready for bed. Devin slept on the fold out couch up front with Bob. Kat slept in the back with me.

I was the only one still sober at bedtime and would probably be the only one without a hangover in the morning. After they bedded down, I checked all the doors and windows then slipped in bed beside Kat. She was fully dressed and nowhere close to being sober. There was zero chance of hanky panky, which was fine with me.

Had it not been for Kat's gorilla like alcohol induced snoring, I would have slept well.

.

Chapter Forty-five

Bob woke me just before six. He's good that way. He knows we usually get up when the sun rises and he sees his mission as making sure I don't oversleep.

Usually, when it's just me in the bed, he'll crawl up beside my face and tap my cheek with his paw until I wake up. But with Kat taking up more than half the bed, there wasn't room for him to get close enough for his paw routine.

Instead of pawing my face, he decided to work on my feet. He started with my big toe, giving it three quick bites. That's all it took to get my attention. I sat up and whispered, "Bob, that's enough. I'm getting up."

He wasn't convinced. He stayed at my feet until I got out of bed. Kat was still asleep and I didn't see any sense in waking her. She had an hour before she needed to get up and get ready to go to Panama City. Both she and Devin would wake with hangovers and I wanted to be out of their way when they got up.

I pulled on my pants and shirt, laced up my tennis shoes, grabbed a towel and my travel kit and headed to the campground bathhouse. I showered, shaved and prepared for the day. When I got back, the girls were still asleep. It was getting close to seven and time to wake them. I figured the best way to do it was to brew up some of the Starbucks instant coffee I'd purchased the night before.

The sound of the microwave woke Devin, who was

sleeping on the couch just a few feet from the kitchen. She sat up, rubbed her head and asked, "What the hell are you doing?"

I held up the Starbucks box. "Making coffee. You want some?"

"No, I want to go back to sleep. Turn that damn thing off."

The bell on the microwave rang, letting me know the water I was heating was ready. I poured about half of it into each of the two coffee cups filled with the Starbucks powder. I stirred the mixture, being sure to make a lot a noise banging the spoon on the inside of the cups. Devin didn't appreciate this but she did get up. She came over, took a sip from one the cups and then headed to the bathroom.

Kat was up a minute later. She walked in the kitchen and asked, "Do I smell coffee?"

I pointed at the steaming cup on the counter. "It's Starbucks. I made it especially for you."

She picked up the cup, took a sip and smiled. "You did good, Walker. I needed this."

She moved over to the kitchen table and sat. "Where's Devin?"

I pointed to the bathroom. She nodded.

For the next thirty minutes, the girls drank coffee and got ready for the day. Devin showered and found some clean clothes in her duffel and put them on. Kat did the same but with her own clothes.

We were almost ready to leave when Kat came over and sat on the couch beside me. She looked at me and asked, "Would it be okay if I rode over to Panama City with Devin in her Bronco? I probably won't get to see her for a long time after this and if I rode over with her, we could talk.

"I'd ride back with you, but you'd have to drive over there alone. Would that be okay?"

I was thinking, *Yeah, it would be more than okay. It'd be nice to have a little peace and quiet on the drive over.* Of course, I didn't tell her that. Instead I said, "Kat, I'd miss you, but I wouldn't be alone. Bob will be with me. He'll keep me company."

She smiled. "Good, I'll go tell Devin."

While she was telling Devin of the new travel arrangements, I went outside and unhooked us from shore power. There wasn't a sewer connection at our site, so I didn't have to worry about dumping the tanks.

When I got back inside, Devin said she and Kat were going to stop at McDonald's on the way out of town. They offered to pick something up for me, but the logistics of me trying to catch up with them while driving the motorhome didn't make sense, so I said, "Don't bother."

Kat said she'd call me as soon as they got to the impound lot and let me know if there was room to park the motorhome close by. Then, without much fanfare, they left.

I took a deep breath, relieved that I'd have some privacy for the next couple of hours. Since I wasn't going to McDonald's, I made my own breakfast. Two strawberry Pop Tarts and a can of Mt Dew.

Smelling Pop Tarts, Bob came up front. He rubbed my ankle, hoping for a treat, but it wasn't to be. No Pop Tarts for him. He huffed his displeasure then headed off to see if the girls had left him anything special.

After breakfast, I took a few minutes to make sure everything was put away and all the cabinet doors secured.

Devin had folded the bed back into the couch and had stuffed the sheets in the overhead compartment. That saved me some work and made it easier to get things ready for the road.

With everything secure, I picked up Bob and held him while I brought in the slide room. I didn't want to risk him getting crushed by the slide as it closed. He seemed to understand it was for his own good, but as soon as the slide stopped moving he wanted down.

With the slide in, all the doors locked and everything stowed away, I climbed into the driver's seat and prepared to go. I started the motor and, while it warmed up, programmed the GPS with the address of the impound lot.

Chapter Forty-six

The drive on US 98 to Panama City from St. Joe was uneventful. Not much traffic until I got close to Tyndall Air Force Base, and even then it wasn't bad.

Devin's trailer had been towed by a private contractor and was held in their impound lot. The previous day, the Sheriff in St. Joe had called and let them know it was okay to release the trailer after Devin paid any fees that were due.

The lot was only a few miles past Tyndall. Kat called me when they got there. She said there wasn't much room on the street to park the motorhome and it would be better if I met them in the Walmart Super Center, about a mile past the East Bay Bridge.

This would keep me from having to fight city traffic and there'd be plenty of room to park the motorhome in the Walmart lot. I could even top off my fuel tanks there before heading back east.

I found Walmart without any problem and was happy to see they had a Murphy gas station with lanes big enough for the motorhome. I didn't see Devin's white Bronco so I headed to the fuel island. We'd driven almost three hundred miles since I last filled and used a little over thirty gallons, meaning I was getting about ten miles a gallon. For a motorhome like mine that wasn't too bad.

I filled the tanks and pulled over to an open area in the lot and parked. I wanted to make it easy for the girls to find me when they showed up. I killed the motor and waited.

Ten minutes later, they arrived. Devin was driving and she was the first one to get out of the Bronco. She walked up to me with a big smile on her face and said, "I got my trailer back. It's in good shape. No scratches or dents and it was still locked up. No one had been inside and the package was there."

She came closer and gave me a hug. While holding me, she whispered, "If you ever get up this way again or if you get the Mango Blues, stop by and see me. I promise I won't make you sleep on the couch."

She kissed me on the cheek and stepped back. "It's been fun but I have to go. The Monkeys are hooking up my trailer and I have to watch over them to make sure they don't mess things up again."

She blew me a kiss, walked over to her Bronco and got in. Kat was still sitting in the passenger seat, talking to someone on her phone. She ended the call, leaned over and hugged Devin. She got out, carrying a small package, and headed my way. Devin drove off, waving when she pulled out of the lot.

Kat came up and handed me her phone. "Daddy wants you to call him. Just press the redial button and it'll connect."

"Call your father? What does he want to talk to me about?"

She shrugged. "I don't know. My guess is it has something to do with this package. He's expecting your call. Don't make him wait."

I pressed redial on the phone and stepped away from Kat. After two rings, her father answered.

He didn't ask how I was doing or where we were. He simply said, "Walker, listen to me carefully. It's important you deliver my daughter and the package she got from Devin to Oscar Scherer State Park today. I want you to go there and set up camp. Then walk with Kat to site sixty-three to deliver the package. You need to do this today, before dark."

He paused, waiting for me to ask questions. When I didn't, he continued. "Do you know where Oscar Scherer Park is?"

I did. I'd driven by it many times. It was on US 41, just a few miles south of Sarasota Florida. About fifteen miles north of Mango Bay in Englewood where I'd been living for the past eight months. Kat had been living there as well, house sitting an empty trailer. I didn't mention this to Kat's father. I simply said, "Yes sir, I know where it is. But I'm not sure I can get a campsite there. The park is usually full this time of year and I don't have a reservation."

"Don't worry about that. I called ahead and reserved a site in your name. When you get to the park, check in. Then drive to site sixty-four and set up like you normally would if you were planning to spend the night. Then take Katrina for a walk and go to the site next door, site sixty-three. Take the package with you.

"But for this to work you have to get to Oscar Scherer today, before dark. If you're late, the gates will be closed and you won't be able to get in. Don't let that happen.

"Another thing, don't tell Katrina where you're going until you get there. Just tell her you're taking her back to Mango Bay. Any questions?"

I could think of several but I had the feeling Kat's father wasn't the kind of guy who would answer them. So I just said, "No sir, no questions."

"Good. Drive safe and get there before dark."

He ended the call.

Kat had gone into the motorhome soon after she had handed me her phone. I was pretty sure she wouldn't have heard anything her father had said to me or anything I had said to him. Even if she had heard my side of the conversation, it wouldn't have given much away.

I stepped into the motorhome and found her sitting on the couch with Bob. She looked tired, maybe from drinking too much the night before or just the stress of the trip.

She looked up. "What'd he say?"

"Who?"

"My father. You were just talking to him on the phone. What'd he say?"

No way was I going to tell her the truth. Her father had made it clear I had to keep it a secret. So I said, "He was telling me that I needed to make sure you stayed out of trouble on the way back. He said under no circumstances were we to stop at the Walmart in Perry. Remember what happened the last time we were there?"

She smiled. "Yeah, I bought a skillet."

"Yes, you did. After you used it to smack some guy upside his head with it."

She smiled again. "He deserved it. But you're right, we better not stop there."

She looked around the motorhome then asked, "I sure wish you'd sell me this thing. If it were mine, I'd be home now."

"That's true. You'd be home now. Speaking of which, you ready to head back?"

"Yeah, as long as I don't have to drive."

I pointed at the passenger seat. "You going to ride up front with me?"

She shook her head. "Not if I can avoid it. I've got a headache. Mind if I sleep in the back while you drive?"

"No, go ahead. If you get bored, come up here and see me."

She went to the back, used the bathroom and then climbed into my bed. When I was sure she was settled in, I pressed 'home' on the GPS. It was set to Englewood, which was about 20 miles south of Oscar Scherer State Park. The route to get to either place was the same. The GPS would show the estimated arrival time—which was important since I needed to get there before they closed.

It would be a four hundred thirty mile drive. If we left right away and didn't make any stops and didn't get caught up in traffic as we passed through Tampa, we might be able to get there before they closed the gates. Or not.

I started the motorhome, put it in gear and got back on US 98 heading east. Bob came up from the back and jumped up on the passenger seat beside me. He looked out the window for a few minutes then decided to take a nap.

I had a feeling he knew we were heading home.

Chapter Forty-seven

Almost as soon as I left the Walmart lot, the GPS wanted me to get off 98 and head north on 231. It showed I could save almost an hour of travel time by avoiding Mexico Beach, Port St. Joe and Apalachicola.

Since the GPS was usually right, I followed its spoken instructions as it took me north. An hour later, it had me turn east on US 20. The road wasn't as good as 98, but there was almost no traffic. I set the cruise control to sixty and we made good time.

We reached Perry three hours later, a little after one in the afternoon. I caught the first red light, which put me in sequence to catch the next three. At each one, I had to come to a full stop, wait two minutes for the light to turn green, and then pull away. About the time I got the motorhome back up to speed, the next light would catch me. After the third one, Kat came up from the back, wiping the sleep out of her eyes. "Where are we?"

"Perry. Your favorite place."

"How long did I sleep?"

"About three hours."

She frowned and tried to clear her throat. "I'm thirsty. You want some water?"

I did.

She went back to the fridge, grabbed two bottles and came back up front. She handed me one and went to sit in the passenger seat until she saw Bob was already there.

"You think he'll scoot over for me?"

"Maybe. Pet him, see what happens."

She gently touched his head and softly pulled one of his ears. He liked that. A lot. He slowly lifted his head to see who was giving the magic touch. When he saw it was Kat, he stood and stretched and then jumped down onto the floor. Kat took his place and patted her lap. "Up here, Bob. Let me do you some more."

He ignored her and headed to the back.

"Is he mad at me?"

"No, he's probably just hungry. He'll be back."

She took a sip of water then asked, "How far we going today?"

I pointed at the GPS. "All the way. If we don't get caught up in traffic we'll be home before dark."

She looked at the GPS then back at me. "But I promised you we'd spend the night in Manatee Springs. Don't you want to do that?"

I did, but it wasn't in the cards. Not today. I was on a mission. I had orders from her father. "Get her to Oscar Scherer before they close." I couldn't tell her that, so I said, "The campground at Manatee Springs is pretty full this time of year. We didn't reserve a spot, so we probably couldn't get in. But that's okay; we'll do it some other time. I'd just as soon keep driving. We're making good time and it'll be nice to get home."

Kat took another sip of water. "Okay, but if you get tired, let me know and I'll drive."

I glanced at the GPS. It showed our estimated arrival time to be five forty-five. We'd lost some time getting through Perry. We couldn't afford to get much further behind if we were to make it to Oscar Scherer before the gates closed.

Going south from Perry on US 98, there wasn't much traffic. I kept the motorhome just below the speed limit, trying to make up the time we'd lost earlier. Things were going good until I realized the bottle of water I'd finished off was now making its presence known. I needed to make a pit stop.

According to the GPS, Cross City was five miles ahead. I'd have to stop there. I asked Kat what she knew about the place. "Do they have a Walmart in Cross City?"

"They used to. But they closed it down."

"What about gas stations? Is there one big enough for the motorhome?"

"Yeah, there's a Marathon station. Only has two pumps but plenty of room for a motorhome. You need to stop?"

"Yeah. Need to get gas. Maybe something to eat too. You hungry?"

"Getting that way. There's a McDonald's next to the gas station. I'm not sure they have anything I'd want. Not today, with the hangover I've got."

I had a cure for her hangover, and it wasn't food from McDonald's. It was a Goody's powder. Acetaminophen, aspirin and caffeine. Wash it down with soda and she'd perk right up. I'd offer her one when we stopped.

I was still thinking about what we could eat when she said, "We still have turkey and cheese in the fridge from last night. I could make sandwiches. Will that work?"

It would.

Ten minutes later, we were sitting in the motorhome

parked on the back side of the Marathon gas station eating turkey and cheese sandwiches with pretzels on the side.

We'd parked facing McDonald's and while we ate we watched the ebb and flow of people going in and out. Most seemed a bit on the heavy side. Maybe that's what prompted Kat to ask, "After we eat, you want to get out, get a little exercise?"

I did. But time we spent outside walking around was time we weren't getting closer to Oscar Scherer. Before I could agree to a walk, I needed to check my phone to make sure we were still on schedule.

We'd left Panama City at around ten and driven two hundred miles to Cross City at sixty miles an hour. By my calculations, it should have been just before two o'clock. But my phone showed it to be three, an hour later. Maybe it was wrong.

"Kat, what time does your phone show?"

She pulled it out and showed it to me. "Three o'clock."

I looked at the display. I couldn't figure out how we'd lost an hour. "Didn't we leave Panama City around ten?"

"Yeah, about then. Why?"

"Because we drove four hours and it should be two o'clock now. But it's not. It's three. Somehow we've lost an hour. How could that be?"

She knew the answer. "Walker, Panama City is Central Time Zone. But we're back in Eastern Time now, so you lose an hour."

I'd completely forgotten about time zones. I'd set the GPS while we were in Panama City, in Central Time Zone. It had shown our Oscar Scherer arrival time in CST.

But we'd moved back into Eastern Time and lost an hour.

Instead of arriving at Oscar Scherer just before six, we'd be getting there just before seven. That meant the gates might be locked—assuming they closed them at six. I decided to check to make sure.

I opened a browser on my phone and pulled up the Oscar Scherer web page. There it said the gates closed at dark. No specific time mentioned. I went to Google and typed in 'sunset today'. I knew the results would take into account the location of my phone. I was relieved when the screen showed, "7:43 PM. EST."

That meant we had almost five hours before the gates at the park were closed and we only needed three and a half hours to get there. Instead of having to rush and worry about staying on schedule, we could take it easy.

I put my phone away and said, "If you want get out and walk, we can. It might be nice to stretch our legs before we get back on the road."

I'd offered her a Goody's powder and she taken one before we had lunch. Now that the caffeine was starting to kick in, she was feeling better. We locked the motorhome and walked around the residential neighborhood behind the station for about twenty minutes.

When we got back, Kat asked if I wanted her to drive. It was nice of her to offer but I didn't need her driving today. I had to be sure we made Oscar Scherer on time and I wanted to be behind the wheel all the way. I couldn't tell her that, so I said, "You can drive if you want but we're heading into Tampa during rush hour. It's going to be real crazy. I'd really rather do it myself."

She laughed. "I was hoping you'd say that. You drive. I'll watch."

We left Cross City and headed south. From there on, it

was smooth sailing until we reached Tampa.

As expected, we got there at the start of rush hour and traffic was crazy. Cars going twenty to thirty miles over the limit and others going twenty under. Crazy, unsignaled lane changes were the norm.

I did my best to stay out of everyone's way. I kept in the right lane when I could and ignored the drivers who blew by me using the shoulder. For locals, this craziness was just part of their daily routine. They were used to driving in rush hour traffic at insane speeds. Not me. It was something I could live without.

I was relieved when we finally crossed over the Skyway Bridge, leaving the worst of Tampa traffic behind us. When we reached I-75, I got over in the right lane, pulled up behind an eighteen wheeler and let him lead the way. Thirty miles down the road we took the Venice exit. We were almost there.

Chapter Forty-eight

The Venice exit road splits when it reaches US 41. One side goes south toward Venice and the other goes north toward Sarasota. The road going south is the one we'd normally take to get home but I'd taken the north road. Kat noticed this and brought it to my attention.

"You missed the turn."

"I know; I did it on purpose. We've got to make a stop before we go home."

"We have to stop? This close to home? Can't you do it tomorrow? I'm tired."

"No Kat, we can't do it tomorrow. It's something we have to do today."

She crossed her arms. "Well, whatever it is, I'm not getting out."

She wasn't happy about making an unscheduled stop but there wasn't much she could do about it.

Three minutes later, we reached the entrance to Oscar Scherer State Park. I slowed the motorhome and turned in. I kept going until I reached the ranger station. There, I pulled over to the side and parked. When I started to get out, Kat asked, "Why are we stopping here?"

I knew she wasn't going to like the answer but she needed to know. "Because we're spending the night."

"What? We're spending the night here? Why? We're less

than ten miles from home. Why stop here?"

"It's a surprise. You'll see."

She shook her head. "I don't like surprises. Take me home. Now."

I didn't. I grabbed the keys, got out and walked up to the ranger check-in station. "I think you have a reservation for me. Name's Walker."

The ranger typed my name into his computer and said, "We do. One of the best sites in the campground. Close to the river and lots of privacy."

He handed me a pamphlet showing things to do in the park, circled the location of our site on a campground map and gave me a card to put in the motorhome window. "You're all checked in. If you need anything, we'll be here until dark."

I thanked him and went back to the motorhome. As soon as I got in, Kat said, "Tell me again why we're here."

I handed her the map to our campsite. "We're camping. That's why we're here. Now, if you don't mind, look at the map and tell me how to get to our site."

"No. I'm not doing anything until you tell me the real reason we're here."

It was time to tell her the truth. Or at least some of it. I turned to her. "When I spoke with your father this morning, he said to bring you and the package to this park. He reserved us a campsite and wanted us to spend the night here. He said after we set up camp, we'd learn what to do with the package."

She shook her head. "He told you not to tell me, didn't he?"

"Yeah, he said not to tell you."

"He's always doing things like this. Keeping secrets."

I started to say, "It runs in the family," but decided against it. She was already miffed at me. No need to poke the bear.

She sighed. "I guess we're spending the night here."

I nodded. "Looks that way."

She looked at the campground map. "We're in sixty-four. Take the next left, go over the bridge and then left again. Our site is at the end of the loop."

I followed her directions and we soon reached site sixty-four. It was a back-in with a gravel pad. Trees all around, giving us lots of privacy.

I drove past it, stopped, put the motorhome in reverse and used the backup camera to ease onto the gravel pad. When I had the left corner of the motorhome lined up with the power pedestal, I stopped. I checked the driver's side mirror to make sure there was plenty of room to run the slide room out. There was, so I went back to the slide panel and pressed the button to extend it. When it was all the way out, I went back up front and killed the motor.

Since it looked like we were spending the night, I went outside and hooked up to shore power and water. When I came back in, Kat was sitting on the couch. The small package Devin had given her for her father was beside her.

She didn't look happy. "What are we supposed to do now?"

"We take a walk. And we take the package with us. You ready?"

"A walk? Are you sure?"

"Yeah, that's what your father said to do. Take a walk and take the package with us."

She stood. "Okay, let's go for a walk."

She picked up the package and we headed out. Her father's instructions were to take her and the package next door to site sixty-three. It would be the first site on our right. We wouldn't have far to go.

I led the way out onto the road and waited for Kat to catch up. The package she was carrying was small, not much larger than a cigar box, and didn't look heavy. Still, I offered to carry it.

She shook her head. "No, I've got it."

I pointed to our right and said, "Let's go that way."

"Sure, why not?"

She wasn't happy, but she played along because she knew this was what her father wanted her to do. We walked side by side and quickly came to site sixty-three. I stopped and nodded at the motorhome parked there. "That's a Coach House. Twenty-three footer with double slides. Looks new. Wonder who owns it."

Kat shrugged. "Looks expensive. Probably someone with a lot of money. "

I pointed at the front bumper. It had a vanity license plate that said, "Mango Blues."

"I wonder what that means."

Kat shrugged again. "I don't know. Maybe they have a cat and it's related to your Mango Bob."

I smiled. "Let's go ask them."

She shook her head. "Don't be silly. We don't want to bother them with a crazy question. Let's just keep walking."

She started to walk away but I reached out and took her hand. "They won't mind. Let's go talk to them."

I figured since Kat's father said this is where we were to

take the package, the people inside would be expecting us. They wouldn't run us off.

I walked to the door, intending to knock, but stopped when I saw a white envelope taped below the door handle. Handwritten on the front was, "For Katrina."

Kat hadn't followed me onto the site. She was still on the road, not wanting to bother the people who were camping here. I turned to her and said, "Kat, come here. There's something here you need to see."

She heard me, but didn't reply. She wasn't sure whether we should be invading someone else's campsite.

I walked out to her and said, "Kat, there's an envelope with your name on it taped to the door of that motorhome. I'm pretty sure it's something your father wants you to read."

She looked at the motorhome. "There's an envelope on the door with my name on it? Are you sure?"

"Yes, I'm sure."

"Are there people inside?"

I shrugged. "I don't know. The lights are on but the blinds are drawn and I can't see in. Whether there are people in there or not doesn't matter. The envelope on the door has your name on it. It's for you."

I headed back to the expensive looking motorhome and this time Kat followed. When she saw the writing on the envelope, she smiled. "That's my father's handwriting."

She took it off the door and pulled out the single sheet of paper that was inside.

"It says I'm supposed to open the package."

Chapter Forty-nine

It had come down to this. Four days on the road, trying to recover and deliver a package to Kat's father. But instead of delivering it to him, we'd been sent to a campsite in Oscar Scherer State Park and instructed to open the package there.

Kat didn't question why she was supposed to open the package. She wasn't going to question her father's instructions. She removed the brown wrapping paper to reveal an ornately carved box made of dark wood. It looked old. A gold colored metal clasp secured the top.

Kat unhooked the clasp and opened the box. Inside she found a set of keys. Under the keys was a note saying, "Unlock the motorhome and go in."

"Think we should?"

I nodded. "Sure, if the key unlocks the door, we're at the right place."

There were four keys on the ring. Two small ones, a larger one with the word 'Ford' on it, and another with a barrel end. She tried one of the small keys first. It fit in the keyhole but wouldn't turn the lock. She tried the second small one and it worked. It unlocked the door.

She turned to me. "You want to go first?"

I did. I wanted to see who or what was in the motorhome. I wanted to learn why we'd spent four days on the road chasing down the package of keys. But I also thought that Kat's father would want her to go in first. I was getting the feeling he had set all this up for her and I didn't want to spoil whatever he had planned.

"Kat, I'll go in first if you want me to, but I think your father would want you to. The note he wrote is addressed to you, not me."

She nodded and reached to open the door. When she pulled the handle, a set of steps slid out from under the coach. The sudden sound of the moving steps caused her to jump back. She instinctively brought up her fists, ready to fend off an attacker. But there was no attacker. Just the steps.

She grinned at me and pointed at the steps. "I didn't expect that. Automatic steps. Way cool!"

I just nodded. I'd seen this feature on a lot of motorhomes. Touch the door handle and the steps slide out. Makes it easier to go in and out.

With her confidence restored, Kat gingerly stepped on the first step. It held her weight and didn't move. Still on the first step, she opened the door, stuck her head in and asked, "Anyone in here?"

There was no response. She waited a few seconds and asked again, this time a little louder. "Anyone in here?"

Again, no response.

She took the second step and then ventured inside. I followed. From where we were standing near the door, we could see there was no one else inside, unless they were hiding in the bathroom or bedroom.

"You want me to check?"

Kat nodded. She did.

I stepped around her and checked the bedroom first, including the closet, then the bathroom and shower. I didn't find anyone. Strangely, there were no personal items in either room. No clothes in the closets, no toothbrushes in the bathroom. No used soap in the soap dish. Nothing to suggest anyone had ever used this motorhome.

The place wasn't empty though. There were place mats on the dining table, clean towels in the bathroom, even dishes in the kitchen cabinets. Everything looked brand new, like it had been staged for a prospective buyer.

Kat walked around and kept saying, "Nice. Nice." Everywhere she looked, it was either, "Wow," or, "Nice." It was clear she was impressed. After checking out the bathroom and bedroom, she came over and said, "This place is amazing. First class everywhere you look. And you know what? It has the same floor plan as yours."

I'd noticed the same thing. The layout was almost identical to my motorhome. The only difference was, instead of having a sofa and a dinette in the living area, it had just a dinette. No sofa.

The lack of a sofa was understandable. The motorhome was five feet shorter than mine; there was no room for a sofa. But with the double slides, it felt larger inside than mine. It was also a lot nicer. Hardwood floors, maple cabinets, Corian counter tops and cream colored ultra-leather upholstery. Very upscale.

I decided to check out the driver's seat. It too was soft, cream colored ultra-leather. Taped to the steering wheel was another white envelope addressed to Kat.

I let her know and she came up front to look at it. She picked up the envelope and pulled out the folded note from inside. As she read it, she started to cry.

"What?" I asked.

She showed me the note. It said, "Katrina, I hope you enjoy your early birthday present. I trust that Walker will help you learn how to set it for camping. He'll find the manuals and the title papers in the overhead bin.

"If you have any questions, call me. And drive safely on your way home."

The note was signed, "Mom & Dad."

The motorhome was a gift from her parents. They knew she'd been looking for one and was frustrated with her lack of success.

Her father had apparently decided this was the one for her. Looking at the paperwork, it appeared he had purchased it from the Coach House factory located in nearby Nokomis, Florida. He'd gotten them to deliver it to Oscar Scherer and then figured out a way to surprise her with it.

Kat was overjoyed. After drying her tears, she pulled out her phone and called her parents. While she was talking to them, I started thinking about what Devin had said to me back in Panama City. Something about getting the Mango Blues.

She said if I ever got them, I should visit her. I didn't know what she was talking about then, but now that I'd seen the Mango Blues license plate on the front of Kat's new motorhome, I had a pretty good idea what she meant.

I whispered to Kat that I was going outside. She nodded like she understood, waved bye, and carried on with her parents.

Back outside, I pulled out my phone and called Devin. She answered on the third ring. "Walker. Let me guess. You have the Mango Blues."

This time I knew what she was talking about. I asked her straight out. "You knew about this all along, didn't you?"

She didn't hesitate. "Of course I knew about it, I planned

the whole thing."

I was surprised by her answer. I figured she would deny everything then make me work to get the truth out of her. But she hadn't. She'd come clean. Sort of. I still had some questions.

"Did Kat know? Was she in on it?"

"No, she didn't know and she wasn't in on it. It was her father's idea. He wanted to surprise her with a motorhome. But he needed time to get it bought, outfitted and put in place. So he called me.

"He said he needed about a week to get everything done and he needed her out of town. So I came up with a plan. And if Dabbo hadn't hired the Trailer Monkeys to move my Airstream, it would have gone off without a hitch."

She paused, giving me time to ask a question. "So Dabbo worked for you. That means he didn't buy the trailer from Fowler in Crystal River?"

Devin laughed. "Walker, I'm surprised you haven't figured it out yet. There was no Fowler. He never existed. There was no fake pregnancy either. I made it all up to move the plan along.

"My trailer was never stolen. I hired Dabbo to play the part of a buyer. His job was to move my trailer to a warehouse. Keep it there for a few days until we found it. But he made the mistake of hiring the Trailer Monkeys. That's when the plan started falling apart. Those fools lost my trailer and things got crazy after that.

"But thanks to you, we got it back on track, losing only a day. In the end, it all worked out."

I sighed. "It worked out for you. Not so much for me. I got beat up in your little play and I still have bruises to show for it. Next time, clue me in before we start."

I knew when I said the words 'next time' I was in trouble. But she let it slide, at least for the moment. Instead, she asked, "Was Kat surprised?"

"Yeah, she was. She really likes it."

"Good, her father will be happy with the way this worked out. It'll be good for you too."

I couldn't figure out how, so I asked. "How will this be good for me?"

Devin had a pretty good answer. "When Kat's father first came to me about this, he specifically asked for you. He said to give you a major role in whatever I planned. He wanted to see how well you handled yourself in these kinds of things. And I gotta say you did an amazing job. When he gets my report, he'll be impressed."

This was news to me. Devin was writing a report about our road trip? And delivering it to Kat's father? I sure hoped there were a few things she was going to leave out. Like our sleeping arrangements. I was thinking about this when Devin said, "Walker, you did good. You were the leading man and played your part well. So well that I've got a part for you in the next one I'm planning. I'll give you a call in a few days and tell you all about it. Till then, stay healthy."

She ended the call.

I put my phone away and walked over to Kat's new motorhome. The door was open, so I went in. Kat was sitting at the dining table, an open bottle of wine and two glasses in front of her. She looked up and said, "I'm glad you're back. There's something I want to show you."

She stepped to the fridge and opened it.

It was packed with food, including what looked like two ready-to-eat gourmet meals and another bottle of wine.

"Can you believe it? They stocked it up with everything I need. Food, wine, cheese, and crackers. There are eggs for breakfast and even coffee for the coffee maker. They thought of everything."

She continued, "So my question to you is will you have dinner with me?"

It was the easiest question she'd ever asked me. The answer was, "Yes."

After dinner, at Kat's request, I showed her how to use the various systems in her new home. Everything pretty much worked the same way as it did in mine, but Kat wanted me to go over it with her so she'd know how to do it on her own.

Once she felt confident she knew how things worked, she said, "If you'll spend the night with me, I won't make you sleep on the couch."

It was an interesting offer, especially since she didn't have a couch. And it was difficult to turn down. But I did. Kat needed to spend the first night in her motorhome alone. It would be the best way to learn how to live in it on her own. If she ran into problems, I'd be right next door, ready to help.

We agreed it would be good for Kat to take her new motorhome out on a one day and back road trip. I'd ride with her just in case she had questions or problems. We decided that the Camping World store on the other side of Tampa would be our destination. It would take three hours to get there, three to get back. The trip would give her experience driving I-75 and give her a chance to pick up any needed supplies at Camping World.

As it turned out, she bought a few things there, including a new set of microfiber sheets for her bed. We broke those in later that evening.

The next morning, Kat headed south to the Florida Keys. She wanted to spend a few days with her family before heading out on her first big adventure. She said something about going to an emerald mine in North Carolina. It sounded like fun, but I'd had enough of the road for a few days, so I headed back to my home base in Englewood.

The first few days back, I cleaned up the motorhome and took care of some minor maintenance issues. I caught up with email, including replying to a few inquiries from potential business clients. It wasn't long, though, before I got bored. I missed the road.

I had my map out and was planning a trip when Devin called. I wasn't sure I wanted to talk to her. Weird things happened when I was around her. But maybe things would be different this time. I took her call.

"Hey Devin. What's going on?"

"Just calling to see if you're ready for another road trip."

I should have said, "No." That would have been the smart thing to say. But sometimes I don't always do the smart thing, especially when it comes to women.

I didn't say no. Instead, I said, "Give me one good reason I'd want to go on a road trip with you."

She gave me three, and I started packing.

Author's Notes

Almost all the places mentioned in this book are real. Details about some of the locations have been invented or enhanced for the sake of the story.

When writing these books, I travel in my motorhome with my bobtailed cat and we visit and camp at the places mentioned in the books. This helps me visualize what I write and gives me a great excuse to get on the road and explore some really interesting locations.

All the characters in my books are fictional (for the most part). But don't be surprised if you visit Florida and see people acting just like the ones in my novels. People like that do exist.

This is the sixth book in the Mango Bob series, and the seventh one will continue where this one left off. There's a good chance the adventure will take us to the emerald mines in North Carolina or maybe the diamond mine in Arkansas. We'll just have to wait and see how it goes.

Thanks for reading!

The adventure continues . . .

If you liked *Mango Blues*, please post a review at Amazon, and let your friends know about the Mango Bob series.

Other books in the Mango Bob series include:

Mango Bob

Mango Lucky

Mango Bay

Mango Glades

Mango Key

You can find photos, maps, and more from the Mango Bob adventures at http://www.mangobob.com

Stay in touch with Mango Bob and Walker on Facebook at: https://www.facebook.com/MangoBob-197177127009774/

45962905R00174

Made in the USA
San Bernardino, CA
22 February 2017